The Attaché Case

Volume 6
Of the Casebooks
of Octavius Bear

*"Alternative Universe Mysteries for Adult
Animal Lovers"*

Harry DeMaio

Paperback ISBN 978-1-78705-246-8
ePub ISBN 978-1-78705-247-5
PDF ISBN 978-1-78705-248-2

Published in the UK by MX Publishing
335 Princess Park Manor, Royal Drive,
London, N11 3GX
www.mxpublishing.co.uk

Dedicated to

GTP

A Most Extraordinary Bear

Acknowledgements

These books have evolved over a long period of time and under a wide range of influences and circumstances. I am indebted to many people for helping to bring Octavius and his cohorts to the printed page. Thanks most especially to my wife, Virginia, for her insights and clever suggestions as well as her unfailing enthusiasm for the project and patience with its author. To my sons, Mark and Andrew and their spouses, Cindy and Lorraine, for helping make these tomes more readable and audience friendly. To Cathy Hartnett, cheerleader-extraordinaire for her eagerness to see this alternate universe take form. To Jack Magan, Dan Andriacco, Paul Bernish and Zohreh Zand for their encouragement and support.

Kudos to Jim Effler, the late Bob Gibson and Brian Belanger for their illustrations and covers. Thanks, of course, to Steve Emecz and MX publishing for giving Octavius et al. a great home

If, in spite of all this help, some errors or inconsistencies have crept through, the buck stops here. Needless to say, all of the characters, situations, and narratives are fictional.

Also from Harry DeMaio

The Open and Shut Case

The Case of the Spotted Band

The Case of Scotch

The Lower Case

The Curse of the Mummy's Case

The Development of Civilization

Volume 6 Part 1

<u>Our Origins</u>

(From "An Introduction to Faunapology" by Octavius Bear PhD.)

*About 100,000 years ago, according to scientific experts, a colossal solar flare blasted out from our Sun, creating gigantic magnetic storms here on Earth. These highly charged electrical tempests caused startling physical and psychological imbalances in the then population of our world. The complete nervous systems of some species were totally destroyed. For example, "Homo Sapiens" lost all mental and motor capabilities and rapidly became extinct. Less developed species exposed to the radiation were affected differently. Four-footed and finned mammals, birds and reptiles suddenly found themselves capable of complex thought, enhanced emotions, self-awareness, social consciousness and the ability to communicate, sometimes orally, sometimes telepathically, often both. Both speech production and speech perception slowly progressed with the evolution of tongues, lips, vocal cords and enhanced ear to brain connections. Many species developed opposable digits, fingers or claws, further accelerating civilized progress. Some others (most fish and underground dwellers) were shielded from the radiation and remained only as sentient as they were before the blast. This event is referred to as **The Big Shock**. It remains under intensive study.*

The Players

- **Octavius Bear** – Mega-sized Kodiak; Narcoleptic war hero; Consulting Detective; Scientist; Inventor; Seeker of justice; Gazillionaire owner of Universal Ursine Industries; Gourmet/gourmand; Somewhat sedentary and grouchy just on general principles.

- **Mauritius (Maury) Meerkat** – Narrator; Assistant to Octavius; Theatrical Agent; African *émigré* with a French-Dutch background; clever with a shady history.

- **Bearoness Belinda Béarnaise Bruin Bear** *(nee Black)* – Gorgeous polar superstar, with the Aquashow, "*Some Like It Cold.*" Wife of Octavius; Extremely rich widow of Bearon Byron Bruin living in Polar Paradise in the Shetlands; Owner-pilot of the last flying Concorde SST.

- **Arabella Bear** – Hybrid bear cub prodigy; Twin daughter of Bearoness Belinda and Octavius.

- **McTavish Bear** – Hybrid bear cub prodigy; Twin son of Bearoness Belinda and Octavius.

- **Frau Schuylkill** – Octavius' beautiful Swiss she-wolf estate manager/cook/pilot/security officer with many other mysterious and military talents. She rescued Octavius from his dive off the Breakurbach Falls while he was struggling with his nemesis, Imperius Drake.

- **Wyatt Where** – Another wolf. Former military intelligence officer who had retired to a security post at the Bank of Lake Michigan in Chicago and then quit to join Octavius.

- **Benedict & Galatea Tigris** – White Bengals – The Flying Tigers – Pilots of Belinda's and Octavius' aircraft – brother and sister.

- **Chita** – Beautiful, fascinating, clever, wealthy, sexy, immoral and highly independent feline who among other things, is the publisher and editor-in-chief of *PURR* and *SOW* magazines..

- **Mlle Woof** – Bichon Frisé – Governess to the twin cubs.

- **The Ambassador** – Rhinoceros – Octavius' client.

- **Joseph** – Dromedary Camel – Majordomo at the Embassy Residence.

- **Major Butho** – Rhodesian Ridgeback Dog – Security Officer for the Embassy and Residence.

- **Doctor Mopsi** – Greater Red Rock Hare – Embassy and Residence Physician.

- **Idi** – Impala – Embassy Commercial Attaché.

- **Madame Leonie** – Lioness – Embassy Cultural Attaché.

- **Boswell Boar** – Boar – Embassy Consul.

- **Charles Gibbon** – Bonobo (sic) – Embassy Deputy Chief of Mission.

- **Oliver Ostrich** – Ostrich – Embassy Press Attaché.

- **Drusilla & Bertha** – Goats – Embassy Maids.

- **Mr. Alex** – Civet – Jeweler Extraordinaire.

- **Faluj** – Impala – Shady Dealer in Diamonds.

Locations

Cincinnati, Ohio; Polar Paradise in the Shetlands;

Washington DC and environs

Octavius

Chapter One

Do Bears give you a scare? Well, me too.

So, I'll pass on this tactic to you.

You just fix that old Bear

With a cold, piercing stare.

But make sure that he's Winnie-the-Pooh.

My boss, mentor, companion and friend, Octavius Bear Ph.D., is an ursine of many personas. *(personae?)* To wit: Mega-sized Kodiak *(9 feet tall and 1400 pounds);* Narcoleptic; War Hero; Polymath Genius; Consulting Detective; Scientist and Engineer; Inventor; Seeker of Justice. He is also somewhat sedentary and grouchy just on general principles. However, no one has ever accused him of being a diplomat.

So, when the Ambassador of a yet to be revealed country called upon him to investigate the suspicious demise in Washington of their commercial attaché, it created a major stir among us minions who toil in in the Great Bear's vineyards. It seems Octavius had taken care of a sensitive personal matter for the Ambassador several years ago, and since said attaché perished on foreign soil, namely the Embassy Residence, it suited the Ambassador to bypass US and local law enforcement and seek Octavius' assistance.

A brief digression. Before we rush breathlessly into our action-packed chronicle, a bit of background and identification of the principal players and locations in this thrilling affair would seem appropriate.

First, may I introduce myself? Mauritius *(Maury)* Meerkat! AKA Octavius' sidekick, *(2 feet tall and 23 pounds)* Born and raised in the Kalahari by a clan of criminally inclined suricates. Oddly enough, meerkat families are called "mobs." We were a mob in both senses of the word. In another story for another day, I will tell you how I was arrested on the island of Mauritius by Octavius and given a choice – work for him or work in the penitentiary. Guess what I chose. Actually, being out here on the straight and narrow, working for a genius who is also a classic pain in the tail has its moments. And as a major participant and narrator-in-chief of this opus, I shall bring those moments vividly to life for you. Modesty is one of my strong points.

As to locations and milieus, the Bear's Lair is a magnificent estate on the northern shore of the Ohio River near Cincinnati, where, in addition to an opulent mansion, he also maintains a state-of-the art laboratory and a Roman Temple hangar for his four aircraft. There is also a missile silo disguised as an Oriental pagoda. *(Don't ask!)* All gifts from a grateful government for very important but top-secret services rendered. Across the river in Kentucky is

Universal Ursine Industries, the wholly owned source of most of Octavius' wealth.

Like a famous detective before him, Octavius keeps bees. From their honey, he produces and avidly consumes some of the finest mead known to animal kind. He has even been known to *(sparingly)* share some of it with specially favored acquaintances.

He has a mate and two cubs. Several years ago, a long dormant romance was rekindled and he married the recently widowed Bearoness Belinda Béarnaise Bruin *(nee Black)*. The fabulous Polar Bear star of the Aquabear Review - ***Some Like It Cold*** - holds court in a castle in the Shetlands, recently reconverted to a top of the line resort and theme park called Polar Paradise. They have separate homes. The Bear's Lair and Polar Paradise. There are legal reasons why she must keep her properties and maintain residence in them to retain her bearonial title. Surrounded by a highly efficient staff, the Bearoness manages her estate; her businesses; her aircraft, especially The Flying Aquabear, the last SST aloft; and bearly controls their two hybrid cubs, Arabella and McTavish. *(A Polar and Kodiak can have offspring. However, it is very rare.)* She and Octavius maintain a supersonic shuttle between their estates.

Back here in Ohio, Octavius is also assisted by Frau Schuylkill, a Swiss she-wolf; Cordon Bleu chef; aviator; sharpshooter; former member of the military and now our mansion estate manager. She joined Octavius after rescuing him from a fall at Breakurbach Falls in Switzerland while he was battling with his nemesis, the now deceased Imperius Drake.

She is the spouse of Colonel Wyatt Where, also ex-military. The Colonel was in Military Intelligence, but resigned while on a bizarre mission to reach alternate universes. He then went to work as the security officer for the Bank of Lake Michigan. He left that job to join Octavius along with a technological genius, Howard Watt, a porcupine and specialist in multiverses, exotic weapons and security.

They and Senhor L. Condor, an Andean telecommunications hyper-whiz, supply Octavius with superior brain and animal power. (Don't forget me!) Enough background and introductions. Let our tail unwind.

Maury Meerkat

Chapter Two

Off we go on another big case,

Flying east at a double-quick pace.

At a strange Embassy,

We're expecting to see

Some poor soul lying dead on his face.

"How come I didn't know about your relationship with the Ambassador?"

"It was highly personal both for him and for me and there are areas *(admittedly few)* where you are better off not being a party to the events."

This conversation was taking place over the phone as I settled my small frame into a large and comfortable seat in the Bear's Twin Otter, one of four fixed wing aircraft in his flying circus. The others are an F-15E Strike Eagle; a V-22 Osprey and a ginormous C-5A named the Ursa Major. The Ursa Major is the only plane in which Octavius, given his size, feels comfortable. He does manage to squeeze himself through the specially modified doors of the Bearoness' SST, but always with some protest. He also has a small fleet of large helicopters used by Universal Ursine Industries and his personal team. All told, a substantial air force.

On the estate, there is a large hangar disguised as a Roman temple and a runway decked out with phony construction equipment and made to look like an interstate highway spur under development. The local airport and the FAA are aware of Octavius' aeronautical exercises and play along with him. His neighbors have nary a clue.

As Frau Schuylkill and Colonel Where spun up the Otter's props, I tried to pry more information out of Octavius who had peremptorily ordered the three of us to Washington National Airport where we were to be met by members of the Embassy staff.

"I assume the Ambassador is simply Mr. Ambassador but does the victim have a name, species and title?"

"He is, was, an Impala, a highly gregarious commercial attaché, whose real name is unknown to me but the Ambassador refers to him as Idi."

"Idi?" I queried

"Idi!!" he rejoined.

"Ah ha," I ah-haed, "An Impala. Could we be talking about Africa?"

"I'm sure the three of you will ferret out all the information you require but let the Ambassador play out his game of intrigue. He is a bit eccentric but highly intelligent and seems very honest by African diplomatic standards."

"So," thought I, "Africa it is."

As we set up for take-off, the sound of the engines made any further conversation impractical. Octavius signed off with his typical, "I'll expect to hear your first report this evening. Tell the Ambassador I will join him shortly."

Time to bring the Wolves up to speed as soon as we levelled out. I lurched my way up to the cockpit and climbed up on the flight engineer's jump seat. The Frau was command pilot for this trip and the Colonel was doing co-pilot duties. After getting squared away with Air Traffic Control, they put the Otter on autopilot with a direct heading for Washington DC.

They both turned and stared at me, eyebrows raised. "So, Herr Maury" said the She Wolf, what's going on and what's our plan?"

"We're investigating the suspicious death of an Impala named Idi"

"Idi?"

"Yeah, that was my reaction when I heard it. He was the commercial attaché for this unnamed but definitely African Embassy. Not sure about the cause of death. The Ambassador believes it was foul play. Since the event took place on the Residence grounds, which is foreign soil, he and his security people have taken charge. No local or US national police involvement. He seems to be a good friend of Octavius and asked for his help. Enter thee and me to be followed shortly by the Great Bear."

"We are being picked up at the general aviation terminal by Embassy employees and taken to the Residence in the Virginia suburbs - the scene of the crime, if it was one. The Embassy itself is in Downtown DC on Embassy Row. Now you know what I know. I guess our plan is our usual one. Fact Finding 101. I'm sure His Bearship will be actively micro-managing, first from the Lair and then at the Embassy Residence."

The Colonel squinted. "I wonder how the Embassy security staff feel about us barging in."

"Get ready for resentment. Oh, one more thing. The Embassy physician performed the post mortem examination. Don't know the results. I believe they are anxious to ship the body back home so I doubt if we'll have any extended access to it."

The Frau growled, "Situation Normal. Something's strange. No, everything's strange! What do we know about the Ambassador?"

"Not much. To quote Octavius: 'He is a bit eccentric but highly intelligent and very honest by African diplomatic standards'"

"That still doesn't explain why he envisions foul play. Unless the victim was obviously strangled, bludgeoned, stabbed, shot, drowned, electrocuted, poisoned or hacked to pieces."

Frau Schuylkill

Chapter Three

The Black Rhinos have horns that are large

And their bodies are big as a barge.

They eat grass, nothing more.

They are pure herbivore.

But get out of their way when they charge.

We were met outside the General Aviation Terminal at 1 PM by a uniformed male Doberman who saluted us and led us to a large SUV *(DC diplomatic license plates - shaded windows.)* At the wheel was a smaller female Doberman. We all participated in the ritual loading of the luggage and the passengers. General purpose words of welcome but no indication as to which Embassy staff they represented. No identifying seals or marks on the vehicle. The mystery grinds on.

After a thirty-minute run on parkways, we turned off onto well paved but definitely suburban roads. A turn to the right and we came upon a gated wall enclosing an extensive and no doubt, expensive piece of Virginia real estate. The gates opened, and we moved along a tree-lined access road of the Grand Manor variety and finally up to a fair-sized mansion. Three floors of colonial style architecture surrounded by well-tended gardens, parking garages and a large open space suitable for landing helicopters. Impressive enough but for those of us who dwell in the Bear's Lair, not that impressive. However, this as yet unidentified country was clearly not without resources.

As the Dobermans removed our *(meager)* luggage and we advanced toward the entrance portico, the oversized reception doors were opened by an officious looking Dromedary Majordomo who began a welcoming speech. He was interrupted by the onrush of a huge rhinoceros, covered in casual robes. The Ambassador!

"Aah, you have arrived at last. Excellent, excellent! Doctor Bear informed me of your itinerary and schedules. Am I correct that you, sir, are Mister Mauritius Meerkat and these two splendid examples of Canis Lupus are Frau Schuylkill and Colonel Where?"

Before we could acknowledge our identities, he barreled on. "Well, I am delighted you are here. I want to get to the bottom of this terrible tragedy as rapidly as possible. I eagerly await your analysis. But where is my hospitality? We have rooms set aside for you and Joseph *(the Camel)* will get your luggage brought up. Have you eaten? No? Well, let us deal with that issue immediately. Joseph, ask Ms. Rathbone to lay on lunch. Meanwhile, let us relax a bit. I believe drinks may be in order. A little fortification before embarking on a grisly task."

We walked through the entrance hall, bedecked with flags, Great Seals (*not that kind*) and statues and portraits of various and sundry national worthies, heading toward what looked like a conference room cum library. A well-stocked drinks table took up one wall. Pointing toward the refreshments, he said, "Please, help yourselves. I have several appointments this afternoon, so I will just have a soft drink."

He finally pawsed long enough for me to interject. "Thank you, Mr. Ambassador. We are pleased to be of assistance. However, our briefing by Doctor Bear was exceedingly brief. We have many questions."

"I'm sure you do! I'm sure you do! Let me apologize for the secrecy but in the world of international diplomacy, confidentiality is all. We are not eager to broadcast the news of Idi's death. With this air of mystery, I am perhaps engaging in overkill. Oh goodness, what a terrible choice of words. Before we begin, let me call in the Embassy Chief of Security."

While we were engaged in pouring libations, he took out a specially designed smart phone and with a surprisingly facile use of his hoof made a connection. "Major? Our guests from Doctor Bear's organization have arrived. Please join us."

"Major Butho has been with the Embassy for years. He and his three-animal staff are charged with protecting the establishments themselves, our employees, vehicles, communications, records and processes. He has a room here at the Residence and at the DC location. He is also the liaison between local law enforcement and the security offices back home. Ah, here he is,"

A grizzled Rhodesian Ridgeback Dog with a wide studded collar entered the room, nodded to the Ambassador and stared in our direction.

"Major, these are the detectives I have requested from Doctor Octavius Bear. Mr. Mauritius Meerkat, Frau Ilse Schuylkill and Colonel Wyatt Where. I want you to work with them in the investigation of the commercial attaché's death. I know you believe it was an accident. I am not so sure and I want a second opinion. They will be joined by Doctor Bear tomorrow. He and his spouse will be arriving by helicopter in mid-morning. Meanwhile, stay for drinks and lunch and then let us go and view the body. I have asked our Doctor to also join us. He performed the post mortem."

The three of us looked quizzically at each other. "He and his spouse?" We knew Octavius was coming but Belinda? I didn't even know she was stateside. Interesting. Maybe she's piloting the helicopter. *(The Bearoness is an accomplished aviator of fixed wing and rotary aircraft.)*

Picking up a crystal bowl of brandy, Colonel Where said, "Mr. Ambassador now that we are here, could you please tell us where 'here' is? What country do you represent?"

"My apologies. This is the Embassy of the Sovereign Republic of Gotu on the western coast of Africa. A little-known country and we prefer it that way. We are a medium sized, peaceful nation surrounded by disorderly and potentially hostile states. Keeping a low profile has served us well for the past seventy years. Our commercial attaché was a native of one of those countries until he became a Gotu citizen. His death, if publicized, might incite riots by perennial troublemakers in several countries, including our own. That is why I want to determine that it was indeed an accident as the Major believes. The way to do that is to have disinterested experts such as yourselves exhaust any possibilities of foul play. In short, I want you to energetically pursue every credible lead to prove a killing and FAIL!"

More drinks and a swiftly served meal proceeded apace. Small talk dominated the conversation. Nothing that could enlighten us further. Finally, the Ambassador signaled Joseph and said, "I believe it is time to view the corpse and visit the scene of his death. His body is in a refrigerated locker below. He was found at the foot of the rear staircase with a broken neck."

Chapter Four

The grey Wolf is from Europe, they say

And the red ones are from USA.

But no matter which kind,

You should keep this in mind.

Stay alert when you hear a wolf bay!

So, that's it. We experts provide credence to the accident theory by being unable to prove foul play. Not crazy about that! Our reputations will be on the line. Octavius' credibility and objectivity will be up for grabs, especially since the Ambassador is a prior client of his. I doubt the Great Bear will buy into this.

Meanwhile, we are going on our inspection tour under the guidance of Joseph, the Dromedary Majordomo and the Security Officer. The Ambassador detached himself, pleading the pressure of important duties. First stop. View the corpse. The Doctor, a Greater Red Rock Hare, met us outside the locker.

Major Butho made the introductions. The Doctor is a Gotu native by the name of Mopsi on assignment to the Embassy. He seemed to have a nervous tic, rapidly flicking his ears back and forth.

"Welcome, detectives. Doctor Mopsi at your service. Shall we go inside? I'm afraid, Mr. Meerkat, you'll find it a bit chilly. I do. That shouldn't be a problem for you two Wolves."

We entered a room that was probably used as a cold-storage locker. It was now occupied by a gurney upon which the body was laying. He removed the sheet covering the cadaver. "You can see that he was a fairly large animal. Still rather young. His neck is shattered and several bones are protruding. Clearly, he crashed head first. There are minor bruises on his right foreleg."

The Colonel asked, "Impalas are some of the surest footed animals in existence. Did you test the contents of his stomach? Any signs of intoxicants or poisoning that might have induced a fall?"

"I did. He did have alcohol in his blood but at a very low level. Probably some wine or aperitif with dinner. I found no traces of common poisons."

"What was the time of death?"

Major Butho spoke up. "We estimate somewhere between ten and one o'clock. His body was found by one of the maids. Isn't that right, Joseph?"

The Camel nodded. "It was Drusilla. Her screams could be heard all through the house. That staircase isn't used all that much. He could have lain there for quite a while before he was discovered."

The Frau shook her head. "I would like to interview this Drusilla after we visit the staircase. May we inspect the body more closely, Doctor?"

The Hare nodded, flopping his ears several times in the process.

Both Wolves ran their paws over the hooves, legs and flanks of the antelope. Then they tested for broken ribs and bruises. Nothing apparent. The victim's face was surprisingly free of any discoloration and only a small amount of blood stained the break points of the neck. Part of his right antler was broken away.

The Colonel asked. "Any idea where the broken piece of his horn is?"

The Dromedary replied, "We searched for it. No luck."

I spoke up, "We understand you want to ship the body back to Gotu to his next of kin."

The Security Officer scratched his ear. "We haven't been able to locate any relatives yet. He was a bachelor. Lived by himself. Traveled a lot. Seemed to like the ladies but had never established any kind of a permanent relationship here or at home. Rather unusual among Impalas."

"In any event," I said, "we'd like to have the cadaver still available for Octavius Bear when he arrives tomorrow. Any problem with that?"

Joseph rumbled, "I know the Ambassador wants the body out of here as soon as possible but since he hired you people, I doubt if he'd object to holding it a bit longer for your employer's inspection, especially since we can't settle on a destination."

"Great! We might also want to make a second inspection, ourselves. Will the body still hold up, Doctor?"

"If we keep it in here, the deterioration will be slowed down by the cold but I can't guarantee it. At some point, shortly, he should be embalmed."

As Octavius would say, "Hmmm!"

We thanked the Doctor and left him outside the locker. On to the staircase!

Chapter Five

It can now, without question, be said,

The Impala is certainly dead.

It's not easy to tell

Why he suddenly fell,

Landing fatally hard on his head.

As we navigated our way from the locker to the first floor and then to the rear staircase, I looked at Joseph and said, "Tell us about Idi. The Ambassador was not very enlightening."

The Dromedary squinched up his lips momentarily, sighed and looked over at the Security Officer. "There is not much to say. He worked primarily at the Embassy downtown and had a small apartment close by. We might see him once a week here at the Residence. He used one of the transient rooms when he stayed over. His car is in the Residence parking lot. As we told you, he was a bachelor. He seldom brought anyone here besides potential clients who wanted to meet, greet and eat with the Ambassador. As far as I can tell, he was quite successful as our commercial attaché."

"Gotu's principal exports are agricultural and minerals. We also have a small automotive industry and clothing trade. We import finished goods, some food and some military equipment. Our army is very small and we have a rudimentary air force. We do have a coastal support service whose primary mission is rescue. We supply the industrial world with rare earths for use in super high technology. They are extremely profitable

"What are rare earths?" I asked.

"Do you want the long answer or the short one?"

"How about something in the middle!"

The Dromedary took in a breath "All right! Just the way I learned it from our embassy sales brochures. Rare earths are chemical elements found in the Earth's crust that are vital to many modern technologies, including consumer electronics, computers and networks, communications, clean energy, advanced transportation, health care, environmental mitigation, national defense, and many others.

Rare earth-enabled products and technologies help fuel global economic growth, maintain high standards of living, and even save lives. Collectively, they contribute to vital technologies we rely on today for safety, health and comfort. All of the rare earth elements contribute to the advancement of modern technologies and to promising discoveries yet to come. Because of their unique magnetic, luminescent, and electrochemical properties, these elements help make many technologies perform with reduced weight, reduced emissions, and energy consumption; or give them greater efficiency, performance, miniaturization, speed, durability, and thermal stability." He took another deep breath.

"There are seventeen in all: Scandium, Yttrium, Lanthanum, Cerium, Praseodymium, Neodymium, Promethium, Samarium, Europium, Gadolinium, Dysprosium, Holmium, Erbium, Thulium, Ytterbium and Lutetium."

The Colonel and I applauded. The camel bowed slightly.

The Frau growled: "You left out Terbium."

The three of us gaped at her. She blushed.

"Why, so I did. Thank you, Frau Schuylkill. Anyway, Idi facilitated both our exports and non-military imports. He had been at it for at least five years. He was very outgoing, as you might expect. You probably noticed he was quite good-looking and he dressed well. Educated in England but hardly a scholar. Travelled pretty extensively to meet the demands of his job."

The Colonel asked, "Did you notice any changes in his recent behavior?"

The Major replied, "As Joseph told you, we saw very little of him here and when we did, he was usually with the Ambassador. You might want to question some of the staff at the Embassy, itself. Of course, unlike Joseph, I spend most of my time at the Embassy but I seldom came in contact with Idi."

I asked, "Why he was here the night he died?"

The Dromedary said, "That was the day of the weekly staff meeting. The Ambassador likes to hold it here rather than at the Embassy. The meeting ends with dinner. Idi was alone with the Ambassador for a few minutes early in the evening before the dinner. Some of the other staff also had private moments with His Excellency. That is common. After that, I didn't see Idi again - alive, that is. How about you, Major?

"I arrived after dinner. I needed to brief the Ambassador on several attempts to hack our computer systems. They failed. Our IT specialists are quite competent in that regard. I didn't see Idi at all."

"Does all the staff stay over after the dinner?"

"No, most of them go home to their families. As Joseph mentioned, Idi is, was, a bachelor. He lives, lived, in an apartment downtown and was always complaining about not being able to park there. I think once he'd found a parking space, he would walk or take a cab to the Embassy. If he stayed here, he could take the morning shuttle directly to the Embassy compound and pick up his car later on the return trip."

The Colonel growled "We'd like a list of everyone at the dinner. Can you also tell us who else stayed over?"

"I'll have to check with housekeeping. They will have a bed tally."

By that time, we had reached the foot of the rear staircase. Dimly lit, running straight down along one wall with a sturdy looking bannister hemming it in. A large decorative urn sat in the upstairs corner. A picture or two on the walls. Clearly, a utility passage. The floor to ceiling vertical distance was about twelve feet. The staircase itself ran about 22 feet – not too steep. An Impala could cover the span in two leaps. The Colonel asked, "Is this the only available light?"

"No," replied Joseph as he hit a switch on the lower wall filling the stairwell with brightness. "There's another switch on the upstairs wall. Turn it on up there. Turn it off down here or vice versa."

Rubberized pads were nailed to each step. The Colonel went down on his front paws and tested each of the pads. None were loose or torn. He tested the bannister. Solid.

I skittered up to the top and looked down. "From the position we believe the body was in and the location of the wounds, it seems most likely he was coming down. If he was going up, he should have fallen over backwards. It's hard to believe that a nimble animal like Idi would have just fallen forward unless he was impaired."

"Or pushed!" growled the Frau. "And there's still another possibility, He was already dead or unconscious and was thrown down to make it look like an accident."

Deadly silence after that one.

"Would he normally use this staircase?"

"It is a bit of a shortcut from the offices and bedrooms upstairs to the exits and you can bypass the formal rooms on the first floor."

The Frau looked at Joseph. "I think I'd like to see the maid Drusilla now. Can you bring her here?"

"You may have to calm her down. She hasn't come near this area since she found the body."

I had come back down the stairs and said to the Wolves. "I think it's time I called Octavius while you question Drusilla. Joseph, do you think she'd be more comfortable talking alone to another female, especially one who is an outstanding chef like Frau Schuylkill?'

"Probably! I'll bring her here. Major, would you mind guiding Mr. Meerkat and the Colonel up to their rooms. All of you please come down later for dinner and a nightcap."

The Colonel wanted to explore Idi's car. "Where can I find the keys to his auto. I assume it's locked if it was parked outside."

"We insist on having a duplicate set of keys for all the staff's automobiles if they are going to park here. Idi left his vehicle here whenever he traveled, which was frequently. I'll get them for you."

"Joseph, before you go. Can you explain something for me?"

"I will try, Mr. Meerkat."

"How does a diplomatic pouch work?"

"It's really rather simple. The diplomatic pouch can be any kind of container for confidential material transmitted or received by an embassy or other diplomatic entity. Some can be quite large. Properly marked, it is guaranteed carriage without inspection or opening by the host country or any other state involved in its passage. It can be a secure substitute for non-priority e-mail. It is supposed to be restricted to embassy business but some staff members use it for personal material. The Ambassador frowns on that but he really doesn't monitor it."

"Does it run on a schedule?"

"It can be used any time but we do have a weekly pouch that arrives on Tuesdays. That's when we have our staff meeting and any of the documents in the pouch may be up for discussion. We send one back out to the capital on Friday."

"Interesting! Thank you!"

Several minutes later, Joseph returned with a diminutive Goat in tow - Drusilla. We left her with the Frau while the Colonel and I followed Joseph first to get the car keys and then up to our rooms.

"Good afternoon, Drusilla. I am Frau Ilse Schuylkill. I am a private detective as well as a few other things like housekeeper and cook for our team. Do you like to cook?"

The Goat was clearly uncomfortable standing where she had found the Impala's body and was looking for some way to get away from the stairs. She also wasn't crazy about being face-to-face with a She-Wolf. "Yes ma'am. I like to cook. For my family, that is. I'm married with two kids. I sometimes make breakfast here for some of the staff. But the Chef would never trust me with any of the formal meals."

"Would it put you more at ease if we talked somewhere else. It must have been quite a shock to find the Attaché's body here. Where can we go?"

"There's a storeroom right next door with a table and chairs. We could go there."

"Good!"

When they had settled down and Drusilla seemed a bit less nervous, the Frau asked, "What time did you find the body?"

"I'm not sure exactly. I'm on the night shift this week and we were making up extra beds for the stayovers."

"I guess you'll have a few more to make up for the rest of our team, if you're around tomorrow. You'll meet a nine-foot tall Kodiak Bear; a gorgeous Polar Bear and her two cubs; a curly haired white dog and two white Bengal Tigers. But I bet you meet a lot of interesting animals here at the Residence."

"Not that interesting! Anyway, I think it was about one o'clock in the morning. We needed some more pillow cases and I took the back stairway down to this storeroom. That's when I saw him. His body was blocking the stairs. His head was on the floor but most of him was still on the staircase. At first, I thought he was just unconscious but then I saw the bones sticking out of his neck and the blood and I was sure he was dead. That's when I started bleating."

"Were the lights on?"

"Yes. I thought that was strange. Usually I have to turn them on when I use those stairs."

"Did you see or hear anyone else."

"No!"

"Were there any packages or papers next to the body?"

"I didn't see any."

"You probably use this staircase a lot. Have there been any other accidents on it recently?"

"I've been here over three years and I don't remember anybody ever falling or slipping. You can ask the rest of the housekeepers."

"I will. One other thing. The Attaché's right horn was broken off. Did you see it?"

"No, but I was so frightened, and I didn't want to touch the body. The broken piece may have been under him or somewhere else. After they led me away, Joseph and Major Butho took the body. I don't know where they put it."

"It's in refrigerated storage. Do you know who cleaned up after they moved him."

"It was probably Bertha. She was on cleanup duty that night."

"I'll ask Joseph to introduce me. Thank you, Drusilla. You've been a big help. That wasn't a very pleasant experience. Is there anything else you can recall or want to tell me?"

"No, but I don't think I'll be using that staircase very much."

Chapter Six

Now it's time for some brief show and tell

Introducing our team's personnel.

And we learn on the phone

Bear's not coming alone.

We'll be seeing his noble wife, Bel.

Since the Colonel and Frau were mates, they were sharing a large bedroom. I, on the other paw, had a smaller room to myself. I joined the Colonel in his digs and invited him to join me while I called Octavius over an encrypted smartphone. Wyatt plugged in a second pair of earphones and a mike while I made the connection.

"**Bear Here**!" roared a deep ursine voice. No doubt, Octavius was seated at his speakerphone. He believes he must thunder at full amplitude to be heard over that device. This from a technical genius. His staff keeps trying to get him to tone it down but to no avail.

"Octavius! Maury. I'll be calling you over an encrypted link so switch phones. Wyatt is here with me. Frau Ilse is interviewing the maid who found the body. She should be joining us shortly."

I made the transition to encrypted mode and waited. Beeps and boops and the Great Bear was on board, this time with a more subdued voice. He opened in typical Octavius style. "Well?"

"Well," I replied and gave him the Washington tourist's version of our progress, or lack thereof. I passed on the Ambassador's remarks about wanting us to pursue every credible lead but fail to prove foul play. He wants it to be called an accident.

There was silence on the other end of the phone and then one of his signature "Hmms." Followed by, "I don't like that. I don't like that at all. Our agreement was to follow the facts wherever they led with no intervention on his part. I'm half tempted to call this off and bring you back."

The Colonel spoke up. "Octavius, there are some things here that are very strange. His Excellency's apparent change of attitude; the state of the Impala's body; no one is quite sure why he stayed over at the Residence that evening. Actually, that's not true. The Ambassador knows but he hasn't seen fit to tell us - yet. It could have been routine. As long as the Ambassador himself or the Treasury of Gotu is paying, I'd like to hang on. My curiosity has been piqued."

Another long paws. "All right. We'll be flying up in the morning."

I chirped, "Who is we?"

"Belinda, the cubs and me. The Ambassador extended his invitation to them to sightsee in Washington while I worked with you on the investigation. Oh yes, I'm sure Mlle Woof will be there to keep an eye on those two rascals. The Flying Tigers will be part of the flight crew although Belinda insists she wants to pilot the Ursa Minor herself."

Before the conversation could go any further, Frau Schuylkill padded into the room. I pointed at the phone and mouthed "Octavius".

She nodded and coming close to the phone said, "Good evening, Herr Bear" in her unique Switzerdeutsch accent. Wyatt gave her the microphone and the earplugs.

"Good evening, Frau. Can you shed any further light on this situation?"

"I had a short interview with Drusilla, one of the maids. She is a Goat. She was still frightened from her experience in finding the Impala's body but she confirmed that he was lying at the foot of the rear staircase with his head and front hooves on the floor and the rest of his body still on the steps. The lights were on. He wasn't carrying anything that she could see. She started bleating and eventually one of the other maids and Joseph, the Majordomo came. They took her away and that's all she remembers. Another maid came in after they moved the body and cleaned up the area."

"Can you interview that maid? She might have picked up something important."

"I will ask Drusilla."

"Joseph has invited us for a nightcap after dinner. I plan to take him up on it and question him further. For example, did the Ambassador put in an appearance when the body was found? Which room was Idi staying in? Did it seem like he was returning there?"

Snorts from the Bear on the other end of the phone. "All right, Maury. See if you can pick up any more clues. As if we had any clues in the first place. I agree with you, Colonel. I don't like the way all this is turning out. I'll see you in the morning. Click!"

"Anyone for a pre-dinner brandy?"

As we file out of our rooms and down the Grand Staircase *(There must be an elevator somewhere.)* let me get you caught up on a few things. You will meet the Bearoness and the cubs tomorrow. Mlle Woof is a Bichon Frisé, a small French, curly haired dog half the size of the cubs, McTavish and Arabella. She is their governess. How she keeps them in line is a mystery but she is definitely in-charge. Octavius also mentioned Benedict and Galatea Tigris, the Flying Tigers, a pair of white Bengal siblings who fly both the Bearoness' and Octavius' aircraft. They will be coming to Washington on the

Ursa Minor as backup crew. That ship gives new meaning to the words "luxury helicopter." Octavius spends heavily on transportation even though he is somewhat sedentary. But what the hell! If you've got it, flaunt it"

We made a semi-grand entrance into the library where Joseph, Major Butho and Doctor Mopsi were siphoning off some VSOP cognac onto crystal dishes.

"Glad you could join us," said Joseph. "The Ambassador sends his regrets. He is tied up in an overseas telephone conference. I have some names for you. Here is a list of the meeting attendees and here are the staff members who stayed over."

"Not many," I said, "I think we'll make a visit to the Embassy tomorrow after Octavius arrives. There are five names on the stayover list including Idi. Were any of these others aware of Idi's death?"

"They may have been. The maids made enough noise to wake up the entire house. The Ambassador has clamped a complete state of silence on the entire staff. He wants this affair strictly controlled and does not take kindly to being disobeyed."

The Major lapped a healthy slurp from his bowl. "Pardon my curiosity but the Ambassador has not been particularly forthcoming with us, either. May I ask you about your backgrounds and about this Doctor Bear?"

I described Octavius' history, personality, skills and the long list of cases he has solved nationally and internationally. I also made mention of his immense wealth derived primarily from his mega business interests - Universal Ursine Industries. The Great Bear does not rely on his cases for revenue. I also mentioned the Bearoness and her independent fortune. Money was not an issue for the Bears. The Ursa Minor would bear that out. They would also meet the unique sibling team of white Bengals – The Flying Tigers, who pilot the Bear's and Bearoness' aircraft. I slipped in a few comments about the cubs to soften the blow when they arrived.

The Colonel and Frau in turn, described their military backgrounds and the cases they had worked on for The Great Bear. I avoided any mention of my ne'er do well early history or how I came to be Octavius' side-kick and simply listed off some situations I had taken care of and various international law enforcement agencies I had assisted. The Major as well as Joseph and the Doctor seemed impressed. I confessed that none of us knew the circumstances that previously brought the Ambassador and Octavius together. They were both reluctant to discuss the subject.

I asked, "When was the Ambassador made aware of Idi's death?"

Joseph replied, "Not until next morning. He had gone to bed and the Major and I felt we had things in hoof for the moment. He was obviously quite disturbed at the news but did not seem to think he should have been awakened."

"Did he view the body?"

"Oh yes! And he gave instructions to have the Doctor do a post mortem; to notify Idi's next of kin and prepare to send the body home. Then he had a change of heart and said he wanted to employ a disinterested investigative team to examine the evidence and circumstances. That's when he contacted you."

"How did you feel about that, Major?"

"Honestly, I was a bit miffed. After all, the Embassy security team are hardly amateurs. However, on reflection, I decided to go along without complaint. We seem to be working well together so far.

The Frau growled and said, "Yes, and we thank you for your cooperation. We'll try to finish our work as rapidly as we can and not exclude you from any of our activities or conclusions."

This was a little white lie and I'm sure the Major realized it as such, but he let it pass. We agreed that dinner seemed to be in order. During the meal, discussion centered on Gotu. All was not as peaceful and prosperous as we were initially led to believe. The Major shared with us that there were several political parties who had combined to foment unrest. The Prime

Minister was hardly popular. There had been no overt acts yet, but the media outlets were quite blatant in their attacks on him. "*A corrupt, incompetent nepotist whose family is draining the Treasury. Luxurious living while the rest of the country is suffering. In the midst of plenty, there are shortages of basic necessities.*"

We also learned that the Ambassador was the Prime Minister's nephew. Another reason why caution and confidentiality were essential. Idi's death will not play well in the press or with certain politicians. Accidental death certified by a world renowned, objective detective team would go far toward averting an upheaval.

"Was Idi a member of the political opposition?"

"It's not clear what he was. He made himself out to be apolitical. He seldom spoke about the government at home and was smart enough not to get on the wrong side of the Ambassador."

All of that would have rated another one of Octavius" "Hmmm's"

After Joseph gave us instructions on breakfast, the Frau went off to track down the "clean-up" maid. Bertha was another Goat.

"Yes, I was on clean-up duty the other night. First, I helped take Drusilla back to her room. Then I went back downstairs. No, I didn't see the body. They had moved it already. There really wasn't much to clean up. A little blood on the rug. And, oh yes. I guess he broke his horn when he fell. They left it there when they moved him. I picked the broken piece up."

"What did you do with it?"

"I think I put it in the trash bin. I'm not sure."

The Frau practically choked. "Please show me!"

Bearoness Belinda
Béarnaise Bruin
(nee Black)

Chapter Seven

If you are a hybrid bear cub,

You belong to a posh aero club

And you leisurely fly

In a craft through the sky

To a city you call Washing-Tub

The thundering sound of whirling rotors echoed across the Embassy Residence compound as an oversized, super-powered helicopter gently settled onto a grassy expanse. Octavius had arrived in style. His latest aerial toy was a true wonder. Behold the AgustaWestland AW101 VVIP glistening in sparkling gold and white with the name Ursa Minor and the outline of the constellation painted along the fuselage. The North Star Polaris was highlighted. With a cruise speed of 157 mph, a range of 517 miles and a five-hour endurance rating, the Ursa Minor made the 400-mile journey from Cincinnati to Washington DC with ease and comfort. Octavius, in true gillionaire fashion had furnished the interior with luxurious seats and fittings, an opulent galley, and had installed an array of navigation, communication, performance and safety equipment that was state-of-the-art plus. Universal Ursine Industries had seen to that.

For all its size and sophistication, the chopper only required a single pilot. In this case, it was his Polar Bear wife, the Bearoness Belinda Béarnaise Bruin Bear *(nee Black.)* As backup, The Flying Tigers - Benedict and Galatea Tigris, two white Bengal aviators, were along for the ride. BUT Belinda was definitely pilot-in-command. Rounding out the assemblage was Octavius himself and their twin hybrid cubs, Arabella and McTavish Bear, accompanied by their governess, the redoubtable Bichon Frisé, Mlle Woof.

The Colonel, Frau and I moved up to the forward door as the huge blades slowly rotated to a stop. The door burst open and out tumbled two brown and white, oversized fur balls followed more sedately by a little white Bichon Frisé, Mlle Woof. "Uncle Maury, Uncle Maury, we're here in Washing-Tub. Are you glad to see us? Hi Frau! Hello Colonel! *(They were a little cautious when it came to Wyatt.)* Momma flew the helicopper all by herself. Poppa just sat and slept."

(Octavius is known to suffer narcoleptic episodes brought about by a self-administered genetic alteration designed to make hibernation unnecessary. Sometimes, they happen at very inopportune moments. For this reason, as well as his size, he does not drive, control aircraft or boats or use dangerous equipment. Nevertheless, he insists he is not narcoleptic. An ongoing debate! We invariably lose.)

Speaking of whom, the rear cargo door opened and a set of stairs folded out, revealing the nine-foot, 1400-pound bulk of the Great Bear as he tried to maintain his balance. The Wolves rushed to give him an assist. I would have ended up flattened if I got anywhere near them.

Joseph approached from the house, somewhat awed by the opulence of Octavius' and Belinda's arrival vehicle. He stepped forward and bowed as Belinda made her way down the forward stairs, leaving the Tigers to batten down the chopper.

"Milady, welcome! We are honored to have you and your family here with us. My name is Joseph, Majordomo of the Residence. We have prepared rooms for you and your companions and have laid out a luncheon for you. I assume the journey was not too wearing. That indeed, is a wonderful aircraft."

"Thank you, Joseph. Actually, I am a bit tired. We came over from the Shetlands a day ago, on my SST and now on to Washington. Yes, the Ursa Minor practically flies itself and is certainly outfitted with every airborne comfort."

By this time, Octavius and the Wolves had joined us. The Camel nodded and said "Doctor Bear, welcome. I am Joseph, Majordomo here at the Gotu Embassy Residence. We are saddened that a death has necessitated your visit but we look forward to your assistance in resolving this issue. As I have mentioned to the Bearoness, we have rooms set aside for your party and will be serving luncheon shortly. The Ambassador will join you at that time."

Octavius drew himself fully erect as was his wont when making or taking formal introductions. Nine feet tall. Intimidating? Usually, but not to an animal very close to his height and weight. In his best resonant voice, he said, "Thank you for your hospitality, Joseph. I am eager to join my advance team and get involved in our research. Is Security Chief Butho available? I would like to confer with him. And, of course, I look forward to seeing the Ambassador."

As the Great Bear spoke, the Rhodesian Ridgeback was making his way from the parking lot to the helicopter, shaking his head in admiration of the awesome craft. He was taken aback when the two white tigers, Ben and Gal, emerged from the forward door and sprang to the ground. A second round of introductions all around, interrupted by the capering cubs with Mlle Woof in hot pursuit. She bowed briefly to the assembly and scurried off after Arabella and McTavish.

Joseph suggested they follow the maids with the luggage and go up to their rooms while we and Octavius spoke to the Major. He left to check arrangements. We would all be called to lunch shortly.

"One thing before we break up," said the Bear. I would like to go to the Embassy this afternoon with my team and you, Major. Is there a ground vehicle in which we can all fit, especially me?"

"We have a large utility van that should do the trick, Dr. Bear. It has conventional seats up front but removable storage and luggage compartments in the rear. You may have to sit on the floor, however."

Octavius laughed. *(Or was that a sonic boom?)* "I often do, Major, I often do! Let's head for the house. I understand that four staff members besides Idi stayed over on the night of his death. We'd like to interview them down at the Embassy."

The Dog replied, "I'll round them up. Meanwhile, before you go to lunch, perhaps you'd like to view the body, if it won't upset your digestion. The Ambassador is eager to ship it back to Gotu. Doctor Mopsi, who performed the post mortem is here. I'll get him to join us."

"Fine!" Turning to us, he asked, "Is that OK with you three?"

Three nods of agreement. We never know what insights Octavius will bring to a situation.

We headed down to the storage locker. Idi's body was a bit worse for wear but essentially the same as we had left him. We pointed out the wounds, and the obvious bone breakage in his neck and right antler.

"Could he have been killed elsewhere and then thrown down the stairs to mislead us?"

I piped up, "That's what the Frau thinks. Don't you. Ilse?"

The Frau was diffident. "A mere theory, Herr Bear. Oh, I located the fragment of his antler. The 'clean up' maid had dropped it in the trash bin. So much for preserving evidence. I haven't had a chance to analyze it yet."

Doctor Mopsi intervened. "I am of the opinion that he was still alive when his neck broke. However, that doesn't mean that he couldn't have sustained the injuries in a different venue. I hadn't considered that possibility till now."

"Do you think we can persuade the Ambassador to hold off on having him embalmed for one more day? I'd like to examine the body more closely."

The Security Chief said, "Actually, since we haven't been able to contact a family or any next of kin, I was going to suggest cremation. It is not very popular in Africa. In fact, it is even taboo in some countries *(Not Gotu!)* but with land becoming increasingly scarce, cemeteries are being looked at with more critical eyes. It might even be easier if the cremation was performed here. I haven't spoken to the Ambassador about it yet but I plan to. He will probably not be happy. He is afraid of an international incident and feels the more people and organizations get involved, the greater the chance of a leak. However, if it can be a quiet cremation, he may change his tune. We should all three talk with him." His smart phone pinged. "We are being summoned to lunch."

Chapter Eight

While she played with her brother at Tag,

Arabella discovered some swag.

On a shelf that fell down,

Almost cracking her crown,

They found twenty big stones in a bag.

The dining room was laid out with one very large circular table and another smaller one on the side for the cubs and their governess. Given the size of several of the participants, the layout was a bit eccentric but effective. The Ambassador had joined the group and took up a lot of room on one side. Octavius balanced him on the other. Belinda sat next to the Bear and the rest of us were distributed rather evenly around the perimeter. Ever the runt in any group, I squeezed my two-foot frame between the Bearoness and the Frau. Sort of an accidental boy-girl, boy-girl arrangement. Joseph stood to the side and oversaw the progress of the meal. The conversation was being dominated by the stentorian voices of the Kodiak and the Rhinoceros, broken occasionally by the loud squeaks and laughs of the cubs.

I leaned over to the Bearoness and said, "I've been here close to two days and I still don't know the Ambassador's name. None of us do. Has Octavius shared that bit of information with you?"

"Only in the last few minutes. It's René Rhino Reynaud. He's French African. That's all I know for the moment, but give me a little time and I will see what else I can unearth."

She turned to the Ambassador who was busily ingesting a large tureen of soup. "Your Excellency, forgive me for asking but is your mate available? I would so like to meet her."

"I am afraid, dear lady, that would be impossible. Alas, I am a widower. My consort passed away several years ago and I have chosen to remain unwed. When I require someone to play the role of Embassy Hostess, I call upon our Cultural Attaché, Madame Leonie, an African Lioness who has been with the Embassy for a number of years. Doctor Bear, I believe you will be speaking to her later in the day. She was one of the officials who stayed over after our staff meeting the night Attaché Idi had his unfortunate accident. You will also meet our Consul, Boswell Boar; the Deputy Chief of Mission, Charles Gibbon; and our Press Attaché, Oliver Ostrich. I am sure they will be forthcoming about that evening. Now, if you will excuse me, I am late for a teleconference. Please stop by when you return from Embassy Row."

As we rose from our seats, the cubs came running over to the Bearoness, "Momma, Momma, come and see what we found in our room. We were playing Hide and Go Seek and Arabella hid in the closet. As she jumped out at me, a shelf fell down and almost hit her. There was a little bag with stones in it. Do you think they're diamonds?" Octavius heard all of this and said, "Show me, little ones, where is the bag now?"

"It's under our bed, Poppa! We didn't want anyone to take it. Can we keep them?" Arabella grabbed Octavius and Belinda by the paws and started to lead them out of the room. The Bear signaled for me and the Wolves to come along. Mlle Woof caught up with McTavish and the parade left the dining room. Wonder of wonders! The cubs had also found the elevator I'd been searching for. Octavius squeezed into the car which was large enough to accommodate a Rhinoceros. Arabella wriggled her way in as well.

Belinda turned to McTavish. "Tavi, where is your room?"

"Top floor, Momma, way over in a corner. Isn't that right Mlle Woof?"

"He is correct, Bearoness. I think our party has taken up most of the available rooms here in the Residence. This one is a bit out of the way. It doesn't seem to be used that often."

"I'll wait here for the elevator to return. The rest of you should probably walk."

At that moment, Major Butho joined us. "The van is ready for our trip to Embassy Row."

I replied, "Come along, Major, we may have uncovered something very interesting. A bag of stones. Maybe diamonds."

Raised eyebrows such as a Rhodesian Ridgeback may have. "Where? Who found it?"

"The cubs, believe it or not. They're staying with their governess in one of the out of the way rooms on the top floor. They found it while playing in a closet."

He shook his head and started to climb the main staircase. The Wolves and I joined him. Belinda moved toward the elevator.

When we had all reassembled at the cubs' room, Arabella crawled under the bed and then backed out holding a black leather bag. "Here, Poppa. There are twenty stones in there. We counted them. Can we have them?"

Octavius took the bag in his massive paws and poured the contents out on the bedspread. "Diamonds? Fakes? Some other kind of stone? Opinions? It seems rather cavalier to leave a bag of real gems like this up on a shelf."

"An unused shelf high in an unused closet in an unused bedroom," said I. "Temporary storage, no doubt. Possibly made necessary by someone's arrival."

"Octavius grunted, "Let's not get ahead of ourselves. We're not even sure what these stones are. Any thoughts on how to check them out? Major, any trustworthy jewelers here in Washington we can turn to?"

Before the Dog could answer, I blurted, "We're on very familiar terms with someone who thoroughly knows her way around the jewelry world. I doubt there's a diamond merchant on earth that she hasn't dealt with."

The Frau laughed, "Of course! Chita!"

Octavius frowned, "Chita! I thought I'd seen the last of that feline reprobate but you're probably right. OK, let's take these stones with us. Sorry, little ones. We're going to need them. Major, why don't we set off for the Embassy. Maury, see if you can get that felonious Cat on the phone."

As we descended to the entrance hall and out the doors to the parking lot, the Major looked at me and asked, "Who is this Chita?"

Let me enlighten him and you, dear reader, at the same time. Chita is a beautiful, fascinating, clever, well-to-do, capable, sexy, immoral and highly independent feline who, at the moment, is the publisher and editor in chief of PURR and SOW magazines for the sophisticated female reader. As you no doubt suspected, she is a Cheetah and she is currently living in London. She is quite wealthy with domiciles in several major cities, oil wells in the North Sea and several investments with the Bearoness. Early in our relationships, she was a cohort of a mad criminal, Imperius Drake, whom we battled in several adventures. They had a serious falling out. *(He tried to kill her. Eventually, she killed him.)* Over time, she has crossed our paths in a wide variety of cases and situations. Her name still appears on the police "Wanted" list in many countries. Despite her checkered past, we are all quite fond of her, except Octavius. He is convinced she is an international menace but, even so, he has tolerated and, I believe, even admired her. Go figure!

Chita

Chapter Nine

Spotted Cheetah's amazingly swift.

It's a truly remarkable gift.

From zero to fifty

In no time. How nifty!

And just think! Not one gear must she shift!

We reached the oversized van. Octavius squeezed into the back and the Frau, Colonel and I took up seats in the front with the Major at the wheel. Time to call England and the one-and-only Chita.

A few back and forth, to and fro connections and reconnections. Finally, the Cat and I were on line. "Hi Chita, Maury here! Long time, no talk! I need some advice and a reference or two. How goes the publishing business?"

"Hey, Short Stuff, good to hear from you. The magazines are going Gangbusters and we're all over social media. How's that insufferable boss of yours? How's Belinda? I keep waiting for her to fly down to London from Scotland. After all, we are partners in a couple of ventures. I assume Polar Paradise and our genetic lab are doing well. Are the cubs driving everybody crazy?"

"Can you switch to Skype so we can see each other?"

"Nothing easier! Hold on. There!"

A beautiful spotted face came up on my screen, complete with her ever-present diamond collar.

"Hiya, Madame Catt! Octavius is Octavius! He and Belinda and the cubs are here in Washington with the Colonel, Frau and me on a very hush-hush inquiry into a rather bizarre death. Can't tell you more than that. However, as part of our investigation, we have come upon a bag full of stones that look to our untutored eyes like rough, large diamonds. If anybody knows anything about diamonds, it's you. I see you have your trademark neckwear on display. Can you give us the name or names of a diamond specialist in or around the DC area that we can trust and who has the expertise to let us know what we have?"

"Well, DC doesn't stand for Diamond Capital of the universe but give me a minute and I'll do a couple of quickie lookups. Meanwhile, how are the cubs doing? I assume they are growing fast and driving Belinda, Octavius and that French governess of theirs up the wall."

"Believe it or not, it was the cubs who found the gems. They're all set to tour Washing-Tub, as they call it, this afternoon."

"I'll check the evening news for incidents. OK, here we go! There's a Civet in Alexandria whom I have dealt with. A real expert. High priced but worth it. He will recognize my name. He can be trusted to be very discreet. Name is Alex. Alex of Alexandria. He knows me as Madame Catherine Catt. Copy down this phone number and e-mail address. A second, equally expert but not as trustworthy individual is an African Impala, Faluj. He might be involved in smuggling blood diamonds."

*("Blood diamond" is a term used for a **diamond** mined in a war zone and sold to finance an **insurgency**, an invading army's war efforts, or a **warlord's** activity. -Wikipedia)*

"I haven't dealt with him directly but he does have a large clientele. I only have a web address. Here it is."

"That's great, Chita. You've been more help than you know. I'll get on Belinda to give you a shout and bring the cubs down to see you. Are you still in a rock group?"

"Only occasionally. Jake is still in town and we howl every now and then. See ya, Short Stuff."

I looked at the team, "We may have a lead here. Another Impala."

The Colonel and Frau both nodded. I'm not sure the Major heard me and I'm certain Octavius had not. He had fallen asleep in the back of the van. Narcolepsy scores again!

Washington traffic was its usual ugly self as we maneuvered our way toward the Embassy. Crawling along at the pace of an arthritic snail, I had some time to look up both Alex and Faluj. Alex had an elaborate website with dazzling illustrations and dazzling prices. Faluj, on the other paw, simply listed his contact points and address – downtown DC. He didn't even mention his services or wares. "Referrals only." Hmmm!

We finally made it to the Embassy and parked behind the building in an open slot reserved for Residence vehicles. I skittered to the back of the van and woke Octavius. "Showtime!"

I opened the rear door and jumped out of the way as he struggled to his feet. The Major came around and guided us through a large utility door, up a flight of stairs and into a reception area. He nodded to the Red Fox seated at the desk and proceeded to introduce us all. "We have appointments with the Consul, Cultural Attaché, Press Attaché and the Deputy Chief of Mission."

"The Consul is available at the moment. I'll buzz Mr. Boar for you."

A medium sized Boar, well dressed with gleaming white tusks, emerged, shook paws and hooves all around and invited us into his office. Promotional photos of Gotu lined the walls along with images of passports and visas. He sat down behind a large mahogany computer desk. Another desk, no doubt for applicants, and a wall full of closets and file drawers took up the rest of the space. The Colonel, Frau and Major took seats at the applicants' desk. I sat on a desk-high cabinet. Octavius stood – erect or barely so. He was squeezed between two chairs, neither of which would have accommodated his nine-foot frame.

The Boar smiled, showing more teeth to complement his tusks. He reminded me of the late and not too terribly lamented Boar who was the Steward at the Bearoness' castle before it reverted to its theme park/resort status as Polar Paradise.

"How can I be of service, Major?"

"I'll leave that to Doctor Bear."

Octavius smiled, baring his large, scary teeth. It looked like we were going to have a dental beauty pageant. All we needed was a couple of smiles from the wolves to make it official. I don't count.

"As you probably know, Mr. Boar, we are investigating at the Ambassador's request, the death of the Commercial Attaché. It seems you were at the Residence the night of his demise. The Doctor estimates he died between ten PM and one AM. What can you tell us about him and that period? First, why did you stay over after dinner?"

"Not by choice. My car was in the shop and the Embassy shuttle was full of staff members leaving the Residence. I live a good distance from this office so I decided I would stay over at the Residence and take the shuttle here in the morning. Then I could pick up my car during the afternoon."

"Did you see or hear anything during that period that could help us determine the cause of Attaché Idi's death?"

"He fell on the rear staircase, didn't he? The room I had was in the front and to be honest, I had drunk a little too much during and after dinner since I wasn't going to be driving. I was out of it and sprawled on my bed from nine o'clock on. Sorry, but I only found out about his death after I returned next day to the Embassy. Not much help, I'm afraid."

"Did you know the Attaché very well?"

"Hardly at all. We only worked together when he wanted to bring someone into the country for a tour or negotiations. Then it was mostly e-mail, visas and other documents."

"Was he involved in any unusual transactions recently?"

"Nothing out of the ordinary that I know of."

I asked, "Mr. Boar, who manages the diplomatic pouch?"

"I do. It's actually not part of my consular duties but many of the documents involve passports or visas so I guess I'm stuck with it."

"Anything unusual about the pouch recently?"

"Not really. Some of the staff are still treating it as their personal courier service. Probably time for another memo from the Ambassador."

"Any idea why Idi was using the back staircase?"

"Well, it is a shortcut from the upper floor to the parking lot.

Octavius looked at us. "Any other questions or comments? No? Well, thank you, Mr. Boar. We might be back to you but for the moment, we're finished. Let's return to the receptionist."

The Red Fox smiled, "Mr. Gibbon is now available, Major."

"Thank you. Will you ask him to meet with us?"

The Deputy Chief of Mission *(second in command)* was named Gibbon but was in fact, a Bonobo. He was casually dressed and his messy office reflected his relaxed manner. After a round of introductions and welcomes, he laughed and said, "Before we begin, let me explain my name. Everyone asks about it. I am a Bonobo but I was adopted as a child by a family of Gibbons in Asia. I didn't realize I was different until they all moved to Gotu to escape persecution. That's when I met other Bonobos but it was too late to change my name. I've lived on and off with both groups. My experiences bridging species prepared me for diplomacy and of course, here I am in the Embassy. But enough about me. I gather you are investigating the untimely death of our Commercial Attaché."

"That is correct, sir." said the Major. "As we understand it, you were one of the five staff members that stayed overnight at the Residence, including Attaché Idi."

"Right! The Ambassador is contemplating a little vacation and he and I spent time after dinner reviewing upcoming events and assignments."

The Colonel asked, "How long was your meeting with the Ambassador?"

"We broke up about ten. I stopped down in the kitchen for a quick snack and a drink and then went up to my bedroom. As Number One, I have a permanent room at the Residence. The others were in transient quarters."

"Where is your room?"

"On the other side of the building from the Ambassador. As the Major knows, we did that deliberately to minimize the impact if the Residence was attacked. A better chance of survival for one of us. In fact, it was your idea, wasn't it Major?"

The Dog nodded.

"Did you see or hear anything that can shed some light on the Attaché's death?"

"Not at all! That stairwell is enclosed and virtually sound proof. The domestic staff use it and they can be noisy at times."

"What was your relationship with the Attaché?

"Paw's length. The Ambassador and I both keep socializing with the staff to a minimum."

"Did he report to you?"

"No, all the Attachés report directly to the Ambassador.

"What did you think of him?"

"A bit too backslappy and gregarious for my taste but I guess it comes with the job. He was good at what he did. Our GDP is growing nicely and part of that is due to his efforts."

"Do you know why he was staying overnight at the Residence?"

"No, I don't. He usually doesn't stay over."

"Any thoughts on what could have happened? We are still trying to determine whether it was an accident or not. Doctor Mopsi only found minimum traces of alcohol in his bloodstream and no signs of drugs."

"I don't know. To my knowledge, we've never had any kind of incident on that staircase before and Impalas are pretty agile animals. It's a puzzle."

The Great Bear agreed. "It certainly is. Thank you, Mr. Gibbon. We appreciate your time and cooperation."

"My pleasure. I'll be interested in hearing your conclusions."

Chapter Ten

Who stayed over the night Idi died?

When we know, it may help us decide.

It's a flip-a-coin call.

Was it simply a fall?

Or a true case of Impala-cide!

As we left his office, Octavius turned to me and asked, "What did Chita have to say?"

I replied, "She gave me two names here in DC. One is an expensive but trustworthy dealer. Mr. Alex, a Civet from Alexandria. I think we'll be able to get confirmation from him on the nature, quality and cost of the stones. Chita has done business with him as Madame Catherine Catt. The other one is very interesting. An Impala who only gives out the barest amount of information on the web. Name of Faluj. Referrals only! I'm willing to bet he has something going with Idi and possibly the Embassy."

"Could be," said the Bear. "Colonel, why don't you contact this Faluj. Pretend you have some 'merchandise' you want to sell. Tell him Idi from the Gotu Embassy recommended you. Let's see if Maury is right."

"Frau Ilse, get in touch with this Mr. Alex. Tell him we are engaged in tracking down some international smugglers and we're operating in secret. We need an expert opinion on the nature, quality and cost of some stones we've uncovered. Use Chita's name. Madame Catherine Catt. Can we meet him later this afternoon or early this evening?"

"Are you OK with this, Major?"

"You seem convinced there's a connection between these stones and Idi's death."

"I'm not convinced of anything. They could be coincidences. I'm not fond of coincidences. Do we know, on the night of the Attaché's death, who was in the room where the twins found the stones?"

"No one. I checked with housekeeping right after your offspring made their discovery. Whoever planted those stones on the shelf wanted an empty room that he or she could readily access. Shall we meet with Mister Ostrich?"

Oliver Ostrich, the Gotu Press Attaché, was out of his room when we arrived. I started to walk back to the receptionist when a very large bird came galumphing up the aisle. "Looking for me?" he said in a half-screech, half boom. "Oliver Ostrich, Press Attaché. Are you one of the detectives looking into Idi's death?"

I acknowledged that I was.

"Well come on back to my press room and we'll talk."

Once again, two-foot me following a super tall animal. As we reached his office, we were all treated to a unique experience. Octavius was standing upright out in the hall. The Ostrich approached him, extended a wing and looked him straight in the eye. Two nine-footers! The bird spoke, "You must be Doctor Bear. I don't get to meet many animals my height. I suppose you outweigh me a bit as, of course, does Joseph and the Ambassador but it's refreshing not to have to stoop to hold a conversation. Come in, all of you!"

"Thank you, Mister Ostrich."

"Please, call me Ollie. Everyone does."

"Well, Ollie, let me introduce my investigative team. You've already met my colleague, Maury Meerkat, and I'm sure you know Major Butho. These two wolves are my highly professional associates, Frau Ilse Schuylkill and Colonel Wyatt Where. They are all top-notch detectives."

"I'm pleased to meet you all. I just came from the Ambassador's office and was told to fully cooperate with you in establishing that Idi's death was an accident. I was also commanded to keep this all under wraps for the time being."

Octavius snorted, "We don't yet share the Ambassador's belief that this was an accident. It's a bit early to come out with final conclusions."

The Bird looked quizzically at the Bear. "So, you think there may have been foul play?"

The Major sighed, "As Doctor Bear said, 'We don't know yet.' I think it was an accident, but these folks were called in by the Ambassador to provide a definitive conclusion."

"OK. So how can I help you?"

Colonel Where, who had been silent up to this point, asked, "How well did you know the Attaché?"

"Pretty well! I issued press releases and advertising material to support some of Idi's campaigns. We also support the Embassy website and blogs. Publicity takes up a lot of my time and energy. The rest of it is taken up answering press inquiries and reacting to Facebook and Twitter trolls, scandalmongers and the rest. We have monthly and emergency briefings for the international press. Some of that should be handled back at Gotu but our connections here are better established and more widely accepted. The Prime Minister has come to rely on us."

"What did you think of Idi?"

"Interesting guy. We both lived out in the fast lane, but he had two sides. Wide open on some stuff but very secretive about other things."

"Like what?"

"He never seemed to lack for money. I know what our Attachés make, and it wouldn't support his lifestyle. I never knew whether he was taking bribes or kickbacks or had some other businesses on the side. He liked expensive stuff - clothes, cars, good food, ritzy apartment. He didn't seem to dote on the ladies and I've never seen him drunk or indulging in drugs. He did gamble, and I assumed that was where his alternate income was coming from. I really didn't care enough to probe too deeply although if it led to a scandal, I was going to have to clean up the mess. At some point, I'm going to have to clean up this mess, anyway. So, I'm hoping you guys can prove it was an accident."

"I understand he was an émigré to Gotu. Did he still have ties to his country of origin?"

"He never spoke about it, but neither would I. Loyalty is an important commodity in our nation. Between us, the current regime has quite a few opponents, but it always has."

"You seem to have known him better than most of the staff. How did he get along with them?"

"He didn't have much interaction with most of them. An occasional tiff with Joseph about some arrangements he wanted for a visiting fireman.

He did a lot of work with the Consul and the Deputy Chief and as best I can tell, got along well with them. What do you think, Major?"

The Ridgeback shook his head affirmatively.

"However, I think you're about to meet with Madame Leonie, our Cultural Attaché. No love lost there. I'll let her tell her own story."

"One last question, Ollie. Why did you stay over after the staff meeting?"

"The Ambassador asked me to meet with him but then at the last minute, cancelled. I decided to have another couple of drinks and get back to the Embassy in the morning. Still not sure what he wanted."

Chapter Eleven

So, our interviews almost are through

And we haven't found much that is new.

Was the dead Attaché

On some other group's pay?

Are we on to a possible clue?

Madame Leonie, the Cultural Attaché and Official Embassy Hostess kept us waiting while she finished a video call with another lioness. Giggles on the other end and more restrained laughter from the diplomat. Finally, she broke the connection. "My apologies, but my sister is a runaway talker. Good afternoon. I am familiar with Major Butho and it takes no great insight to assume that you are Doctor Octavius Bear. I have never met a Kodiak before. You are, indeed, large. I notice that you are all males. Is it beyond a female's capabilities to be a detective?"

Octavius replied, "Quite the contrary, Madame. Two more members of my team are here but are currently out investigating another possible lead. They are mated Wolves – male and female. Frau Schuylkill is a truly formidable animal. A highly skilled pilot; estate manager; detective;

sharpshooter; security specialist and Cordon Bleu chef. I think you would find her highly intelligent, courageous and physically daunting. She has won several high military awards for bravery. Her contributions to our work are always most valuable."

I followed through, "Another member of our group who represents the finest in capable females is Doctor Bear's Polar Bear consort, Bearoness Belinda Béarnaise Bruin Bear *(nee Black.)* Wealthy in her own right, she owns and manages a spectacular resort and theme park in the Shetlands and is part owner of a state-of-the-art genetics lab. She is the star of the world renowned aquatic show and revue – *Some Like It Cold.* She is also an exceedingly proficient aviator who just completed the journey from Scotland to their US home in Ohio in her own Concorde SST. She then flew from Cincinnati to Washington in a highly sophisticated helicopter that is currently on the grounds of the Gotu Residence. On top of that she is the mother of two rare hybrid cub prodigies. A truly exceptional Polar. I hope you get a chance to meet both these ladies."

Turning her golden eyes in my direction and possibly sizing me up as a mid-afternoon snack, she asked, "And may I know who you are, sir?"

"I am Mauritius Meerkat, Madame, an associate and confidant of Doctor Bear's. As I'm sure you know, we are investigating, on the Ambassador's behalf, the death of Idi, the Commercial Attaché."

"Ah yes, Idi. Idiot is more like it."

The Bear stared at her, "I take it you were not fond of your colleague."

"Colleague, indeed. He didn't know the meaning of the word 'collegiality.' No, I was not fond of him. He went out of his way to impress everyone in sight with his importance. After all, he was bringing revenue into Gotu's coffers while I was draining them with cultural events, educational programs, art, music and literature. He formed an alliance with the Press Attaché to ensure he got most of the media coverage while my efforts went to the back pages, if at all. He was constantly parading himself in front of the Ambassador and the Deputy Chief. I have reason to believe he sabotaged several of my programs and saw to it that I had to fight for every penny I needed to do my job."

She continued, "Now, you're going to ask me if I hated him enough to do him in and the answer is a categorical NO! I may have fantasized about it. After all, in our dark history, Impalas and Antelopes were once the natural prey of the Leonine species. No longer! But I can dream. Anyway, I thought it was an accident."

My turn, "It may well have been, Madame. That is an important question we are attempting to answer."

Octavius: "May I ask, Madame, why you stayed on at the Residence after dinner on the night in question?"

"Well, Doctor Bear, as you may know, in addition to my cultural duties, I am also saddled with being the Ambassador's Hostess. After dinner, I held a meeting with Housekeeping and the Majordomo to plan the month's social events. That took us until well after midnight."

The Major asked, "During that time, did you see or hear anything unusual that might have a bearing on this case?"

"A couple of slammed doors that could have come from anywhere. No shouts, screams or bumps in the night. We were in the library using the household computers. The Deputy wandered in, sandwich and drink in paw, apologized and wandered back out."

"Is there anything else you'd like to tell us?"

"Nothing, except I hope the government sends us a cooperative replacement with a better diplomatic personality and appropriate skills. I'm tired of playing tug-of-war." Without a further word, she turned back to her computer screen and left us to make our way out. I would have looked back over my shoulder if I had one. "Well, there's a happy camper!"

The Development of Civilization Volume 6
Part 2

It's Elementary - Diamonds

(From "An Introduction to Faunapology" by Octavius Bear PhD.)

Diamonds are renowned for their extraordinary physical qualities, caused by strong bonding between their atoms. They have the greatest hardness and thermal conductivity of any material. The word comes from the ancient **Greek** – *adámas* "indestructible".

GIA, The non-profit Gemological Institute of America categorizes diamonds by color, cut, clarity and carat (weight)

Color: In addition to the clear, colorless gems that make up most jewelry, some impurities may color diamonds blue, brown, yellow, green, purple, pink, orange and red. The famous Hope Diamond is a deep blue. Diamonds also can disperse light of different colors.

Cuts and shapes: Cut refers to the symmetry, polish and proportioning of a diamond. The cut of a diamond greatly affects a diamond's brilliance. The finer the cut, the greater the brilliance and fire of the diamond. Shapes include round, princess, pear, marquise, oval, heart, emerald, baguettes and cushion.

Clarity is a metric that grades the visual appearance of each diamond. The less inclusions and blemishes, the better the clarity grade.

Carat (ct.) refers to the unique unit of weight measurement used exclusively to weigh gems and diamonds. It is not necessarily indicative of size. The Hope diamond has a weight of 45.52 carats.

The hardness of diamonds also makes them an ideal material for industrial use in cutting and grinding tools. As the hardest known naturally occurring material, diamonds can be used to polish, cut, or wear away any material, including other diamonds. Common industrial applications of this property include diamond-tipped **drill bits** and saws, and the use of diamond powder as an **abrasive**. Less expensive industrial-grade diamonds, with more flaws and poorer color than gems, are used for such purposes.

The market for diamonds has been dominated for decades by the DeBears group. *(No relation.)* Unfortunately, until recently there has also been a brisk trade in blood diamonds that we have described previously. Several other groups round out the major sources of gemstones.

Most natural diamonds are formed at high temperature and pressure at depths of 140 to 190 kilometers (87 to 118 mi) in the Earth's **mantle**.

Minerals containing carbon provide the source, and the growth occurs over periods from 1 billion to 3.3 billion years. Diamonds are brought close to the Earth's surface through deep volcanic eruptions by magma.

Diamonds can also be produced synthetically in a High Pressure High Temperature (HPHT) method which approximately simulates the conditions in the Earth's mantle. An alternative, and completely different growth technique is chemical vapor deposition (CVD).

Several non-diamond materials, which include cubic zirconia and silicon carbide and are often called diamond simulants, resemble diamonds in appearance and many properties. Special techniques have been developed to distinguish natural diamonds, synthetic diamonds, and diamond simulants. One characteristic leading to diamond identification is its superior thermal conductivity. Electronic thermal probes are widely used in the gemological centers to separate diamonds from their imitations.

Then, of course, there is the Chita sniff-test which unerringly succeeds in identifying the real thing.

Chapter Twelve

Are the stones in the bag real or fake?

There are tests we should carefully make.

If it turns out they're real

With a good jeweler's seal,

There are several steps we will take.

We ran into the Colonel and Frau as we crossed the reception area.

"Herr Bear, Mr. Alex is waiting to see us. Major, can we get over to Alexandria before the traffic goes wild?"

"I think so. We can talk on the way over. Did you have any luck, Colonel?"

"Did I? This Faluj character is straight out of pulp fiction. He's also not the brightest gem in the necklace. I recorded the call. Let's get settled and I'll play back my conversation. What happened with the lioness?"

I replied, "Definitely not an Idi fan but she has a pretty good alibi for the time in question. You know, I'm beginning to lean a little more toward the accident theory. I think we're going to discover that some jewelry smuggling was going on but it may not have been connected to Idi's death.

The Bear snorted, "I hate coincidences."

"Me too!" said the Colonel. "Wait till you hear this call. Idi was a smuggler or a courier."

He plugged his smart phone into the van's speaker system.

The conversation follows:

Ringing phone.

"Yeah!?"

"Mr. Faluj?'

"Who wants to know?"

"My name is Marvin Wolf and I have some merchandise I think you might be interested in. I was referred to you by Idi at the Embassy."

"Oh yeah. How is Idi?"

"Things are a bit quiet for him right now."

"Well, tell him I expect to hear from him. Tell him it's that time of the month. Now what can I do for you?"

"As I said, I have some uncut goods from Africa that I'm interested in selling. Twenty stones, to be exact."

"What about weight and quality?"

"I'll leave that up to you to decide"

"Do they come from the same source as Idi's shipments? Those are always first class."

"I have my own source. I lost my buyer and I'm looking for a new contact. Interested?"

"Since you're a friend of Idi's, I'll take a look at what you've got. They better be good. I don't carry crap! When can you get here?"

"Not until tomorrow."

"OK! Here's my address."

The Colonel cut off the recording. "I hope he doesn't wait for me tomorrow. Well, that sheds some light on our Attaché's activities."

Octavius grunted, "It certainly ties him to the bag of diamonds but it still doesn't explain his death. Are we getting anywhere near Mr. Alex's establishment, Major?"

"Just a few more minutes, Doctor Bear. I'm eager to find out if these stones are high quality and what they're worth. Frau Schuylkill, what did you tell Mr. Alex?"

"First, I dropped Chita's name, sorry, Madame Catt's name. He recognized it. It seems he has shops in several countries. He has done business with her in Paris and London. Then I told him who we were and that we were working on a hush-hush assignment for a foreign government involving diamonds. We needed an expert assessment for which we were willing to pay. But under no circumstances was he to reveal any of this to anyone. Was he willing to work with us on that basis? He was. He expects us right about now."

(Now being 4 PM.)

As she was speaking, the Major pulled up in front of a very fashionable boutique. Alex of Alexandria. He told us to go in and seek out Mr. Alex while he found a parking space.

The four of us walked into a very well-appointed shop with display cases aglitter with jewelry in all shapes and sizes. Diamonds, sapphires, rubies, emeralds, pearls, bracelets, earrings, necklaces and a wild assortment of exotic pins. Tiny spotlights played on the sparkling gems. Frau Ilse looked very interested. What female wouldn't be. Subdued music in the background. A fashionably dressed white Arctic Fox, wearing a few sparklers herself, approached us but seemed a bit taken aback by Octavius' size and the fabulous coats of the two Wolves. She practically fell over me. *(It happens a lot.)*

"Good afternoon, Lady and Gentlebeasts! Welcome to Alex of Alexandria's. How may I be of service?"

The Frau smiled, showing her hundred or so perfect teeth. "Good afternoon, I am Frau Ilse Schuylkill. We have an appointment with Mr. Alex."

"Mr. Alex will be with you in a moment. Is there anything I can do or show you?"

"Thank you, no. Could you let him know we are here? Another member of our party, a Rhodesian Ridgeback Dog will be joining us as soon as he finds a parking space.

"Of course! Please be seated! *(She looked askance at Octavius' girth.)* Or feel free to wander about. I think you'll be very impressed with our selections."

I was impressed. No wonder Chita dealt with him. Nothing second class for that cat. Speaking of cats, a Civet in a tail coat, emerged from behind a mirrored door and skittered toward us. *(Cat is a misnomer. They are more like Racoons.)* He bowed to the Frau. "Frau Schuylkill? Wonderful, wonderful! And these are your associates? Please come back with me to our workroom."

Once again through the mirrored door. The Frau made the introductions. There was an old German Shepherd wearing a loupe, seated on a workbench, carefully grinding a large ruby.

The Civet went over to him and whispered in his ear. The dog nodded, took off his loupe, shut down the grinder and carefully placed the ruby in a sample box. He went over to a wall safe and deposited the box on a shelf, closed the door and spun the dials. He bowed and left the room.

"Now we are alone," said Mr. Alex. "Let us view these stones you want me to appraise."

At that moment, the door opened and the Major stepped in. The Frau introduced him without referencing his duties, profession or employer. The Embassy was not to be mentioned.

The Civet climbed up on the workbench, took an empty sample box and put on his own personal, gem encrusted loupe. Octavius untied the bag and poured the stones into the box.

"There are twenty in all. If you can also tell us their provenance, that would very helpful."

"Hmm, let us see. I have a diamond testing device here that will check their specific gravity and thermal conductance among other things. Yes, I'm pretty sure these are diamonds. Let me test the whole batch."

One after another, he zapped each stone. The indicators on the tester consistently rose and the device beeped. "Frau Schuylkill, you have twenty genuine diamonds. As to quality, their clarity is high and I can see no serious occlusions. Their color is very fine. Their ultimate value will be determined by how they are cut, of course. In the paws of a reliable and skilled jeweler, each stone of this size should bring in $5,000 to $10,000. Maybe more. Of course, in the rough, the price would be about a third to half of that number."

"As to provenance, it's difficult to say. I have not seen these types of stones on the controlled market. I would be guessing, but there is a good chance these are blood diamonds. I wouldn't touch them."

"Thank you very much, Mr. Alex. That was most helpful. Because of our confidential status, we will pay for your services in cash. Remember, please. This session did not take place."

"I was pleased to help. Please give Madame Catt my best regards and remind her that Mr. Alex is always at her disposal with new, exciting and legal offerings."

Chita would no doubt respond to the 'new' and 'exciting.' I'm not sure what she would think about 'legal.'

After making the confidential payment, we filed out to the van under the puzzled and watchful eye of the Arctic Fox.

"Well, it would seem our friend Idi has been trading in contraband precious stones for a while, if Faluj is to be believed. Two Impalas. I wonder if they were related."

"They could well be, Maury, but all of this still doesn't explain his violent death. Any theories? Although I hate theories. I much prefer facts. Why was this bag of stones poorly hidden in that empty room?"

The Colonel growled. "I don't think it was intentional. If it was Idi, he may have been trying to get away from someone. Getting rid of evidence? That may also explain his fall. He was on the run. But why?"

"Any thoughts, Major?"

"I have always suspected Idi of playing fast and loose. He seemed to have more money than his diplomatic salary would provide. I don't think all his trips were on Embassy business. He didn't drink much. He may have been gambling, although I can't prove it. Someone or something may have caught up with him."

"Let's have one more look at his body when we get back to the Residence," said the Bear.

"What are we looking for?"

"I don't know, damn it."

Chapter Thirteen

While the cubs run and frolic and play,

Mlle Woof watches them night and day.

But addressing her, please,

Do not say Bichon Freeze!

Her name's French and its Bichon Free-zay!

It was about six o'clock when we returned to the Residence. The Major let us off and drove around the back. The Colonel joined him. He wanted to look at the Impala's car. As we came through the door, we were attacked by two high energy, brown and white, fur covered missiles. "Guess what! Guess what! We went to Washing-Tub! Ben and Gal hired a car and took us over there. Mlle Woof came too, didn't you?"

The Bichon nodded her head and gave a rapid wag of her tail.

"We went to the Washing-Tub Monument. It's a big basilisk."

"Non, mes petits. It is an obelisk. A basilisk is a mythical giant serpent. Don't you remember you saw an obelisk when you were in Egypt."

"Yeah, but this one is way bigger. We couldn't go up in it, though. The elevator is broke. But we saw the Capital and the White House. That's where the President of America lives. Poppa, are we Americans?"

Belinda laughed, "Poppa is American and I'm Canadian and Scottish so that makes you international stew."

Arabella giggled. McTavish was all seriousness. "And then we went to the Air and Space Museum. They had a whole lot of old airplanes and rockets. We saw The Spirit of St. Looie and the Wright Brothers' Fryer. Ben and Gal knew all about them. Poppa, you and Momma have a lot of new airplanes and helicoppers and rockets. Why don't you open a museum so everyone can see them?"

"Afraid not, son. We use them too often. Museums are for valuable old things that are being saved and protected. Maybe someday, one of our planes will go on display but not yet. Now, it's time for you two to get ready for dinner."

"What are we having?"

The Bichon yipped at them. "Something good, but you're not getting any unless your paws are nice and clean. Allons!"

Belinda looked at us and said, "I have some news for you. While you were gone, the Impala's body was removed and taken to a crematorium."

Octavius was not happy. He looked at me and said, "Find Joseph!"

The Majordomo was in the dining room supervising dinner preparations. I asked him to come with me. He gave a few instructions to the servers and walked with me into the library where Octavius had taken over a large leather couch. The Wolves were seated across from him. The Bearoness had gone to supervise the ceremony of the washing of the paws.

The Dromedary nodded and asked, "How may I assist?"

Octavius said, "I thought we agreed to keep Idi's body for one more day. We wanted to inspect it again. What happened?"

"The Ambassador decided that we had kept it long enough and since we had nowhere to send it, he told Dr. Mopsi and me to find a cooperative crematorium who would dispose of the body without asking any questions. Dr. Mopsi knew of one here in Virginia. We had the body taken there this afternoon and the Doctor verified that it was incinerated. I am sorry that you weren't consulted."

"Where is the Ambassador?"

"Unfortunately, he is at a state reception and dinner at one of the DC hotels. He intends to stay there overnight."

"Please set up an appointment for me with him first thing in the morning. Very important."

"Certainly, Doctor Bear. Is there anything else I can do for any of you?"

"Joseph, I just realized that you too were in the house when Idi met his fate. Can you tell us your whereabouts during the hours of ten and one AM?"

'I was with Madame Leonie in the library planning next month's events."

"Is it safe to say you did not take a liking to Idi?"

"I had no real feelings about him one way or the other. Let's just say he was not my type of animal. A little too flashy and loud for my taste.

"Who assigned the rooms for the stay-over guests last evening?"

"I did, with Housekeeping's help."

"Did any of the support staff have any problems with him? Any grievances?"

"None that I know of. He didn't stay here that often."

"Is there anything you might want to add to help us sort this out."

"Nothing I can think of at the moment. If I remember anything I'll be sure to tell you. Meanwhile, dinner will be served in an hour. Cocktails are available now."

That sounded good to me. It'd been a long, hard day. It looked like it was going to be an even harder night.

The Colonel came into the room. "I just got finished looking at Idi's car. A late model, high performance convertible. Way above his paygrade. Tucked away in the glove compartment, with the registration paperwork, were several receipts for electronic funds transfers. Never to the same address. Amounts in the thousands. Kind of stupid on his part if he was trying to hide a money laundering operation or blood diamond sales. Nobody said he was smart. Just too clever for his own good. I can't believe the Ambassador or the Major knew nothing about this.

The Bear harrumphed. "I agree! We'd better get ourselves freshened up for dinner. Frau Ilse, did you bring the mead in from the Ursa Minor?"

"Of course, Herr Bear. As soon as you landed."

Chapter Fourteen

The Great Bear mounts a hostile onslaught,

And the Ridgeback resists, as we thought.

It is not a surprise

That he keeps telling lies.

In a web of untruths, he is caught.

Another delicious meal proceeded on schedule. The cubs were being their riotous selves despite Mlle Woof's best efforts. The Flying Tigers had joined us.

Belinda looked over at them and said, "Ben and Gal, thanks so much for taking the little ones in paw. They really enjoyed themselves in Washing-Tub."

Galatea growled, "So did we, Bearoness. They are so smart. It's really scary. But I guess that comes from their parental genes. By the way, we were really impressed with the way you managed the Ursa Minor."

"Don't be. That ship really flies itself. It's a wonder. But I hogged the controls. On the way back, I'll turn the cyclic and collective joysticks over to the two of you. Octavius and I want you both to be proficient in every one of our aircraft."

The Embassy Deputy had been at the Residence during the day and had stayed for the meal, sharply curtailing any discussion of the case. He looked at Octavius. "Any progress?"

"None we can rejoice about. Still fact finding."

"Please keep me posted."

The Major sat down with us.

Octavius leaned over to him. "Major, do you plan to stay over?"

"No, but I can be available if you wish."

"I want to spend a little time with my team immediately after dinner but then we'd like to have a discussion with you. Is 8:30 OK?"

"Fine!"

We waited while Octavius polished off a mini-keg of mead and looked hopefully at Frau Ilse. She disappeared and returned with a refill. We headed up to his room and spread ourselves around on the opulent furniture. Belinda joined us.

"Tavi", she said, "I know you wanted to keep it a secret but it might help if we knew what you did for the Ambassador earlier on."

The Great Bear shifted in his seat, looked up at the ceiling and grunted. "This is very confidential. You asked about his mate. Unfortunately, she committed suicide or so it appeared. It was never fully confirmed. He called me in to investigate under a cloak of secrecy. I was reasonably sure she had taken her own life and told him so. That was the end of it. Now he has me assessing another mysterious death. I'm not the least bit comfortable with this. I plan to face down the Major when he joins us. He and the Ambassador have not been playing straight with us. I'm going to reel out a scenario for him and see how he reacts."

"In fact, I have all but decided to withdraw from this case. Frau and Colonel, prepare to go to the airport and take the Twin Otter back to Cincinnati tomorrow morning. Same with the Ursa Minor, Bel. Alert the Flying Tigers and get the cubs and Mlle Woof on standby. Maury, fly back with us on the helicopter."

That was fine with me. A little aeronautical luxury is right up my alley.

"Maury, let's discuss the diplomatic pouch. I think that's the way those diamonds made their way to the Embassy and to Idi. He would then dispose of them, probably with Faluj, take a commission and send back the proceeds, probably to someone in Gotu but we can't be sure. I think the money makes its way back a different way. Probably electronically. I don't know to whom. Let's see what the Major has to say about that."

There was a knock on the door and the Rhodesian Ridgeback shoved his snout in the opening. He looked around at the assemblage and said, "It's 8:30. Are we meeting?"

Octavius boomed, "Yes. we are! Come in, Major. Would you like a drink?" He gestured toward the Colonel who was seated next to the beverages table. Wyatt held up a bowl and a bottle of Scotch. The Major nodded. Refills all around. Octavius took a healthy slug from his mead keg. "Wonderful stuff, mead. Do you like it?

"I don't think I've ever tried it."

"You should. I'll leave you a sample."

This was overdoing the sociability. Octavius seldom parted with any mead. Personally, I prefer fermented coconut milk VSOP. I should have brought some along.

"We've been trying out a scenario here, Major, and I'd like to bring you into our discussion."

"Fire away!' *(Little did he know!)*

"Major Butho. I don't think you've been telling us the truth. Or you've been letting us wander around in blind alleys while you knew all the time what happened to Idi."

"I resent that. I've been giving you my full assistance since you came here."

"But that full assistance has been misleading. Let me try this on. You and the Ambassador have known for months that Idi was using the diplomatic pouch to smuggle in materials that had high fungibility. Gold, other precious metals, rare earths, diamonds. He would dispose of them and after taking a commission for himself, he would send the money back to someone in Gotu or elsewhere, but not using the diplomatic pouch. Probably some form of electronic funds transfer. You allowed this to continue in the hope that you could trap that someone on the other end but he or she kept eluding you."

"You finally decided enough was enough and resolved to close the traffic off by shutting Idi down. This past Tuesday during the staff meeting, the diplomatic pouch arrived as usual. During a break, Idi got to the pouch and extracted the bag of diamonds we have been toting around. He scooted up to the top floor and left the bag there on a shelf in a remote, empty room where he could pick it back up after the meeting broke up. He got back in time to take part in the discussions. Are you with me so far, Major?"

"Speculate away, Doctor Bear. This is fascinating!"

"However, things went awry for our Impala friend. The Ambassador told him to stay on for dinner. He wanted to discuss a few pending contracts with him or some other business. This didn't fit Idi's plan for a quick exit, diamonds in hoof. Nevertheless, he hung on. He couldn't leave the Residence early without arousing suspicions and that could destroy his profitable game."

"Sometime around ten o'clock, I guess, the Ambassador finally sent for the Impala. You were in the office with him. The Ambassador faced him down with what you knew and what you surmised. You accused Idi of being a traitor, using the money to support a clandestine group planning to overthrow the government."

"You have been reading too many spy novels, Octavius."

"Maybe I have, but here we get to the climax. Idi, not the most courageous individual, panicked. He bounded from the office with you and the Ambassador in hot pursuit. Neither one of you could possibly keep up with an Impala. Very few animals can. He raced down the back staircase and that's when you or the Ambassador threw a large metal object, perhaps an urn, at him, sending him hurtling down to the bottom and breaking his neck and his antler. That's why I wanted to re-examine the body. I wanted to look for traces of paint or metal on his pelt."

"Cremation made that impossible, as you well know. I'm sure you carefully disposed of the heavy weapon just as you did the body. However, Frau Schuylkill got the maid who cleaned up the area after you moved the corpse to show her the horn fragment she picked up and put in the trash. Sure enough, paint and metal fragments in the scratched-up surface. We have that piece of the antler. I'll be happy to show it to you and the Ambassador."

"The Ambassador was right when he called me in. This was a killing. This was no accident even though he wants me to certify that it is. A repeat of a service I performed for him before."

The Dog looked at The Great Bear quizzically. "I don't understand."

"No, and you won't, but the Ambassador will when I see him tomorrow morning. You know, all this drama and stagecraft is ridiculous. If you want to admit to killing Idi, do so. The two of you can invoke diplomatic immunity. If you want to continue with the fable about accidental death, go ahead but you will not receive any certification to that effect from me or my team. No objective and disinterested attestation. We are resigning from this assignment and leaving in the morning. At least my cubs got to see Washington or Washing-Tub as they call it. A rather expensive bit of tourism. Thank you for your hospitality but not your assistance. I don't expect you to break down and admit my scenario is correct but you may want to review the proceedings with His Excellency. Please feel free to react."

"I will. I have never heard such a pile of arrant nonsense in my life. When you and your team first arrived, I had heard so much about the famous

Octavius Bear and his associates that I was willing to set aside any resentment I may have had at being upstaged. I expected to be overwhelmed by a brilliant show of investigative legerdemain. A true genius! Bah, humbug! Go to the Ambassador. Try your cockeyed theories on him. Go ahead and resign. At least we won't have to pay you."

The Dog lapped up his Scotch, stood up and strutted out of the room.

The Colonel laughed, "Well Octavius. I don't know who gave the more dramatic performance. He or thee. Personally, I like your version. Not because you're my employer but it holds together. We probably would have never found the weapon. I suspect Joseph may also be in on this. I suppose, at this stage, you don't care. Anyway, the Frau and I will be out at the airport early in the morning, ready to bring the Otter home."

"Thank you, Colonel. Comments from anyone else?"

"I've heard a few rumors that the current government of Gotu is not long for this world. Idi may have had strong personal ambitions for a major job in the new regime assuming his side won. His smuggling and financial finagling gave someone a boost. That same someone will not be happy at his death. No wonder the Ambassador wanted to play it down and use us as a smokescreen. An accident certified by the Great Octavius Bear and his all-star team of detectives."

"Probably, Maury, probably!"

Thump! Octavius fell over in a deep narcoleptic sleep. As we know from experience, it's impossible to move him while he's out. He'll wake up eventually.

Chapter Fifteen

The Ambassador knows that we know.

The Impala sustained a great blow.

We refuse to opine.

So, it's time we resign,

Leaving diamonds and horn as we go.

Morning at the Residence. I was gulping down a bowl of coffee and waiting for Octavius to stir himself. The Wolves had already left for the airport to retrieve the Twin Otter and fly it back to the Bear's Lair. Belinda and Mlle Woof were busily packing up the cubs' belongings.

"Momma, why can't we have that bag of diamonds? We found it."

"This time, there is no finders' keepers. Those stones belong to the Embassy *(not literally true)* and your father is going to return them to the Ambassador. You stay here with Mlle Woof until I call for you. I'm going out to the helicopter with the Flying Tigers and check it out. We're going to have to make a refueling stop before we fly to Cincinnati. Then, we're going to stay at the Bear's Lair for a few days. You'll love it there. You'll meet Senhor L. Condor again. Remember, Arabella, he rescued you in Egypt. And there's Doctor Howard Watt. He's a porcupine. He knows everything about everything."

"Like you and Poppa."

"Well, maybe, and oh, yes, Marlin, the Dolphin will be there. You met him at Polar Paradise. Now he's at Cincinnati working with Poppa and his team and the technical animals at Universal Ursine Industries to make an underwater language translator. He'll be coming back later to the Shetlands and Polar Paradise to appear at the Aquashow along with Otto, The Magnificent. *(An Otter with truly remarkable talents.)* Many of the Aquabears will be there. There's lots of fun in store for you. Now, help Mlle Woof get you all packed up."

Ta-Da! The Great Bear has made an appearance. I guess he has foregone breakfast. He seems to be in a somewhat belligerent mood. The Ambassador is in for it.

"Come on, Maury. I'm going to resign this engagement. I want a witness to this meeting. Bring the fragment of the Impala's horn. They can bury it along with his ashes. Belinda, get ready for a quick departure. You two, don't give Momma any trouble. We'll be going for another long helicopper ride in just a while."

Off we went to the Ambassador's office. His secretary announced us and we entered. He was not alone. Major Butho was seated in a chair opposite his desk, nervously scratching his ear.

"Good morning, Octavius. I believe you have some news for me."

"If you wish to call my resigning from this assignment 'news,' I suppose I do"

"And good morning to you, Mr. Meerkat. Major, don't be boorish. Acknowledge our guests."

The Ridgeback grunted in our direction.

"The Major has told me about your interpretation of Idi's death and my involvement. I must say I've always admired your intelligence, Octavius. But I didn't realize you had such a wild imagination. So, you think the Major and I killed the Attaché and then conspired to pull off the ultimate cover up by bringing you in to objectively and thoroughly declare it an accident. Do you honestly believe I would spend our country's or my own money so foolishly?"

The Bear growled, "It would not be the first time."

"Ah, the suicide! I see! You are sensing a pattern here, digging up bygones to support your speculation. How impulsive of you and wrong!"

"Your Excellency, we have clearly reached an impasse here. I will not continue in this charade. I hereby withdraw myself and my team from this investigation. There will be no record or correspondence to you or others besides this written notice of resignation." He placed an envelope on the diplomat's desk. "Upon reading it, you will notice there is no conclusion, no mention of cause or explanation for my action. Mr. Meerkat is here to witness this event, if ever a witness is required. Thank you and your staff for the hospitality you have shown to me and my companions. If you would care to have Joseph make up a bill for our transportation, housing and meals, I will be happy to pay it."

"Hardly necessary, Octavius. Needless to say, I am disappointed in you and how this all turned out. Fortunately, I will be leaving for a short vacation in the next few days and I can relax and put this out of my mind."

The Great Bear turned to me and said, "Maury, will you leave on the Ambassador's desk the one part of Idi that wasn't cremated? Thank you. A fragment of the Impala's antler, complete with metal scratches and paint. A souvenir, Your Excellency."

He then reached into his utility belt and pulled out the bag of diamonds. "I am not sure who is the true owner of these gems. I certainly am not. They were found on Embassy grounds by my two cubs but they also have no claim. Since these diamonds, no doubt, traveled in the Embassy's diplomatic pouch, I leave them in your care. The Major can tell you about them." He dropped them on the desk next to his letter of resignation and the antler fragment.

The Ambassador smiled and said, "I sincerely doubt we will meet again, Doctor Bear. Let me wish you good fortune in your future endeavors. I will not thank you for your efforts."

"I do not wish for any thanks, your Excellency. I bid you and the Major a 'good day.'"

Rising to his full height, he strode toward the door. I grabbed my tail and followed suit.

"I wonder where those diamonds will end up, Octavius."

"I think you know as well as I do."

Down the Grand Staircase, past the flags, seals and portraits and out the Ceremonial Door. Pawsing long enough to thank Joseph and bid him farewell, we headed toward the Ursa Minor. The helicopter's rotors began to turn as the Bear, none too gracefully, entered the large cargo door at the rear. He managed to close the door behind him and settle into an oversized lounge seat designed especially for his height and bulk. As usual, he had a great struggle with the seat belts. I squeezed past him, went forward and sat down next to the Cubs, who were chattering and gazing out the windows at the Residence. Those seats were smaller and I could manage the shortened restraints. It's not easy being Meerkat size.

With a roar of the engines, we rose, circled the building and headed off, first to refuel and then on to The Bear's Lair in Cincinnati. In the rear, I could hear Octavius loudly snoring.

Epilogue

A strange letter arrives in the mail.

And it closes this mystery's trail.

For it quite tersely said

The Ambassador fled

And my friends, that's the end of our tail.

Two weeks later: Frau Schuylkill came into Octavius' office carrying the day's mail. I was sitting near his desk sorting out bills, incoming payments and the occasional request for assistance.

"Herr Bear, there is a letter here from the Gotu Embassy Residence in Virginia. Do you suppose they decided to charge you for our stay, after all?"

Octavius replied with one of his famous "Hmmms" and took the letter from the Frau. Slicing the envelope with a letter opener awarded to him by The Ursine of the Year Committee, he looked at the single page and then let out a snicker.

"Here Maury, read this aloud."

The stationery was formal and expensive with the embossed Embassy logo on top. The typed message read:

Dear Doctor Bear:

Since your recent visit here, a few things have taken place that I feel you might want to know.

First, a few days after your departure, the Ambassador went on vacation to a small Central American country.

At the same time, a bloodless coup was taking place in Gotu, resulting in a complete regime change. All the diplomatic staff in the US have been recalled, including the Ambassador. As I understand it, he has chosen to stay in his Latin American retreat, ignoring the new government's calls for his return. Gotu does not have an extradition agreement with the country where he is residing. It is rumored that Major Butho has joined him. I cannot confirm that.

I have been instructed to stay on to facilitate the diplomatic transition. At the moment, only the household staff and I occupy the Residence and the Embassy is closed until further notice.

I thought you might find this of interest. I hope you, your family and associates are well. It was a pleasure hosting you,

Your Obedient Servant

Joseph Kamel Dromedary

Majordomo - Gotu Embassy Residence.

I chuckled, "Well, what do we make of that, class?"

The Frau shrugged and then laughed.

The Great Bear snorted. "I guess a few friends of Idi may be hanging around back home waiting for the Ambassador to return. They may even be part of the government. Ah well! It's a shame this case never took place. Thank you, Frau. Is there any mead available?"

The End of Volume Six of

The Casebooks of Octavius Bear

The Attaché Case

About the Author

Harry DeMaio is a *nom de plume* of Harry B. DeMaio, successful author of several books on Information Security and Business Networks as well as the six volume *Casebooks of Octavius Bear*. A retired business executive, consultant, information security specialist, former pilot and graduate school adjunct professor, he whiles away his time traveling and writing preposterous articles and stories.

He has appeared on many radio and TV shows and is an accomplished, frequent public speaker.

Former New York City natives, he and his extremely patient and helpful wife, Virginia, and their Bichon Frisé, Woof, live in Cincinnati (and several other parallel universes.) They have two sons, living in Scottsdale, Arizona and Cortlandt Manor, New York, both of whom are quite successful and quite normal, thus putting the lie to the theory that insanity is hereditary.

His e-mail is hdemaio@zoomtown.com

You can also find him on Facebook.

His website is www.octaviusbearslair.com

His books are available on Amazon, Barnes and Noble, directly from MX Publishing and at other fine bookstores.

Also from MX Publishing

MX Publishing is the world's largest specialist Sherlock Holmes publisher, with over a hundred titles and fifty authors creating the latest in Sherlock Holmes fiction and non-fiction.

From traditional short stories and novels to travel guides and quiz books, MX Publishing cater for all Holmes fans.

The collection includes leading titles such as *Benedict Cumberbatch In Transition* and *The Norwood Author* which won the 2011 Howlett Award (Sherlock Holmes Book of the Year).

MX Publishing also has one of the largest communities of Holmes fans on Facebook with regular contributions from dozens of authors.

www.mxpublishing.com

Also from MX Publishing

"Phil Growick's, "The Secret Journal of Dr. Watson", is an adventure which takes place in the latter part of Holmes and Watson's lives. They are entrusted by HM Government (although not officially) and the King no less to undertake a rescue mission to save the Romanovs, Russia's Royal family from a grisly end at the hand of the Bolsheviks. There is a wealth of detail in the story but not so much as would detract us from the enjoyment of the story. Espionage, counter-espionage, the ace of spies himself, double-agents, double-crossers...all these flit across the pages in a realistic and exciting way. All the characters are extremely well-drawn and Mr. Growick, most importantly, does not falter with a very good ear for Holmesian dialogue indeed. Highly recommended. A five-star effort."
The Baker Street Society

www.mxpublishing.com

Also from MX Publishing

The Missing Authors Series

Sherlock Holmes and The Adventure of The Grinning Cat
Sherlock Holmes and The Nautilus Adventure
Sherlock Holmes and The Round Table Adventure

"Joseph Svec, III is brilliant in entwining two endearing and enduring classics of literature, blending the factual with the fantastical; the playful with the pensive; and the mischievous with the mysterious. We shall, all of us young and old, benefit with a cup of tea, a tranquil afternoon, and a copy of Sherlock Holmes, The Adventure of the Grinning Cat."
Amador County Holmes Hounds Sherlockian Society

www.mxpublishing.com

Also from MX Publishing

The Detective and The Woman Series

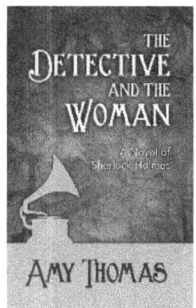  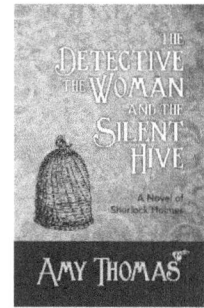

The Detective and The Woman
The Detective, The Woman and The Winking Tree
The Detective, The Woman and The Silent Hive

"The book is entertaining, puzzling and a lot of fun. I believe the author has hit on the only type of long-term relationship possible for Sherlock Holmes and Irene Adler. The details of the narrative only add force to the romantic defects we expect in both of them and their growth and development are truly marvelous to watch. This is not a love story. Instead, it is a coming-of-age tale starring two of our favorite characters."
Philip K Jones

www.mxpublishing.com

Also from MX Publishing

The Sherlock Holmes and Enoch Hale Series

The Amateur Executioner
The Poisoned Penman
The Egyptian Curse

"The Amateur Executioner: Enoch Hale Meets Sherlock Holmes", the first collaboration between Dan Andriacco and Kieran McMullen, concerns the possibility of a Fenian attack in London. Hale, a native Bostonian, is a reporter for London's Central News Syndicate - where, in 1920, Horace Harker is still a familiar figure, though far from revered. "The Amateur Executioner" takes us into an ambiguous and murky world where right and wrong aren't always distinguishable. I look forward to reading more about Enoch Hale."
Sherlock Holmes Society of London

www.mxpublishing.com

Also from MX Publishing

Sherlock Holmes novellas in verse

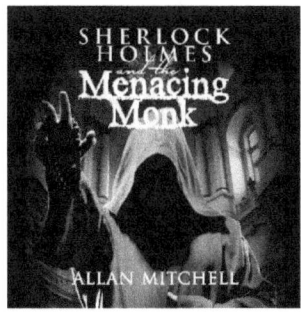

All four novellas have been released also in audio format with narration by Steve White

Sherlock Holmes and The Menacing Moors
Sherlock Holmes and The Menacing Metropolis
Sherlock Holmes and The Menacing Melbournian
Sherlock Holmes and The Menacing Monk

"The story is really good and the Herculean effort it must have been to write it all in verse—well, my hat is off to you, Mr. Allan Mitchell! I wouldn't dream of seeing such work get less than five plus stars from me…" **The Raven**

Also from MX Publishing

When the papal apartments are burgled in 1901, Sherlock Holmes is summoned to Rome by Pope Leo XII. After learning from the pontiff that several priceless cameos that could prove compromising to the church, and perhaps determine the future of the newly unified Italy, have been stolen, Holmes is asked to recover them. In a parallel story, Michelangelo, the toast of Rome in 1501 after the unveiling of his Pieta, is commissioned by Pope Alexander VI, the last of the Borgia pontiffs, with creating the cameos that will bedevil Holmes and the papacy four centuries later. For fans of Conan Doyle's immortal detective, the game is always afoot. However, the great detective has never encountered an adversary quite like the one with whom he crosses swords in "The Vatican Cameos."

"An extravagantly imagined and beautifully written Holmes story"
(Lee Child, NY Times Bestselling author, Jack Reacher series)